I Belong on a Warning Label

Benjamin Kalb

BRIGHTON PUBLISHING LLC
435 N. HARRIS DRIVE
MESA, AZ 85203

I Belong on a Warning Label

Benjamin Kalb

Brighton Publishing LLC

435 N. Harris Drive

Mesa, AZ 85203

www.BrightonPublishing.com

ISBN 13: 978-1-62183-594-3

Copyright © 2021

Printed in the United States of America

First Edition

Cover Design: Tom Rodriguez

Photographer: Shane O'Neal

Model: Sarah A.

"I Can Make Love Disappear.
For My Next Trick I'll Need a Volunteer."

~Warren Zevon

C♪Chapter One♫⊃

YOU COULDN'T HANDLE ME
EVEN IF I CAME WITH INSTRUCTIONS

There were my bare feet on the center of his face. My Smith and Cult white toenail polish looked delicious if I do say so myself. I had manipulated my feet into that position. But he wasn't complaining and neither was I.

It would be over in about three minutes, twenty seconds. The poison on my soles was kicking in and he just laid there licking them, not realizing what was about to happen.

"Your feet smell like vanilla ice cream but taste like orange sherbet," he said. "It's nice."

I thanked him and let him continue.

I learned this form of execution when I was a kid. My mom had bought me a $300.00 chemistry set from Scientific Kids for my birthday when I was eight. One day I was mixing some colorful chemicals together from the set and added a few pesticides from our garage. The next thing you know I accidentally spilled some on the sidewalk and the neighbor's cat licked it up and…well, as you can guess, died.

1

His name was Allen or Adam or something like that. Nice enough guy despite being a lawyer. Met him at a party. I liked his sense of humor and his knowledge of politics, so I invited him to my high-rise condo with a view of the Las Vegas Strip.

"You're a bright guy. Do you believe in God?"

"What? Why Ask Me That Now?" He was still licking my bare soles.

"Either there's a God or there's not. Just by asking someone if they believe in a God means people have doubts that a God exists. No one asks if you believe in baseball, sex or death. They are there for all to see, feel or touch. So is God here with you right now?"

"Absolutely."

"Are you sure about that?'

"I'm sure."

"If there is such a thing as a God, it better save you pretty soon. I had poison on the bottom of my vanilla-smelling, orange sherbet tasting soles, and I'm afraid, even though I've enjoyed every minute of our relationship, you don't have much longer to live."

He tried to get up. He couldn't. His pupils started getting bigger, kind of like an empty stare. His throat locked up. And he laid there very peacefully and died. I lovingly rubbed his forehead with the back of my hand and kissed him on the cheek.

I read somewhere that when you kill someone, your body turns cold. Maybe that's what they mean about being cold blooded. But I didn't feel any coldness in my body. I was regular body temperature. It was business as usual for me.

Adam was the first to go this month. No guns, no knives, no motorized sawblades. I don't believe in violence. Just some creative fatal ingenuity.

Yeah, I know what you are thinking. Who is this sicko who belongs in prison or in some contrived Netflix ten-part series?

Actually, I would make a great wife or girlfriend for the right guy. Really, I mean it. I love kids. I'm kind to animals. I donate to attend charity events every chance I get. I know people would have their doubts about me if they knew how many people I've said good-bye to. Maybe someday I'll get caught. But right now I love my alternate life as a twenty-six-year-old serial killer.

One thing you should know about me up front is I'm honest. I was once engaged to be married. Had I ended up getting married, I'd probably have one or two kids by now, and maybe I wouldn't be doing all these senseless murders. Or maybe I still would. Moot point now. If you watch these TV shows all serial killers were either abused or alcoholic, or their parents abandoned them or some such artificial we-need-to- think-up-something-to-give-the-plot-a-sense-of-depth-bullshit. I wasn't abused. I had a nice childhood. Good grades in college. No drug or alcohol issues. I don't think the world is out to get me. I don't hate men. I don't hate anybody really.

I need the feeling of power, control, or what I call out-smarts. The use of my brain to trap someone into a final submission. A submission not by choice but by desire. I love it. I find it dangerous. Deliciously dangerous. Other than that, I'm a normal girl next door.

The first thing you are thinking is that I need help; that I need to see a psychiatrist. Maybe they need to put me away with a warning label attached to my forehead.

3

So, I'll tell you about the time I went to see a psychiatrist. I paid for six sessions in advance.

Cash. I walked in with a mask over my face, one of those Lucha Libre masks but very feminine. Pink in color. The psychiatrist said he wouldn't see me unless I took off the mask but I told him that with the information I was about to give him I needed to keep it on. I told him it was safer for him not to know who I was. So he reluctantly agreed. For the next five weeks I told him of several of the men I killed. One at a time. I told him that I know it's wrong to kill someone, especially without a good reason, but I enjoyed it. I enjoy creating different, distinctive ways I can end someone's life.

"I admit it. I have an addiction," I said to him.

The first four weeks, I don't think he believed me. He thought I was some dingbat who made up stories. He was more interested in finding out about my childhood and how my parents raised me. I told him I was telling the truth.

During our session in week five I told him that to me it was a feeling of power that I could control someone's life like that.

"They enter the arena thinking they can get the advantage sexually. I either let them have their way with me or they don't ever leave alive. A tap out for life."

Other than that, I'm normal. No hang-ups except I like to change my hair color every once in a while. Now it's light brown with blonde streaks. A couple of months ago it was blonde. After going into detail on three of my earlier homicides, I got the sense he started to believe me. By the time we got to the sixth session, he pretty much knew my life and I guess you can say death story. I asked him an open-ended question.

"Can you solve my problem?"

"Do you want it solved? If you know it's wrong, it's wrong," he said. "You don't need my help. You are only thinking of your own self-gratification." He said I was selfish, and not thinking that I was hurting the moms, dads, sisters, brothers, and former school friends of the people I had killed. He called me a "psycho" and made a faux pas by telling me, "You're good at killing people. Shit, I mean, you're killing good people who have done nothing to harm you. God help you."

There's that God thing again. Why do some people rely on God to solve their problems instead of solving them themselves? I don't think God solves anything other than giving someone a chance to rationalize that some inanimate object will take care of everything that happens in their lives.

The psychiatrist, who looked about fifty years old, wasn't going to last till the end of the session. When I walked in, I gave him an apple as a going away gift. I told him I enjoyed our month and a half of intimate conversation. After three bites of the apple, he was temporarily unconscious. I then tied him up with these little pink tie wraps I usually carry with me and then I put a pink sweat sock in his mouth. My sweat socks had already been dipped in one of my chemical concoctions. I thanked him for his time, and told him he had only a few minutes left on this earth.

"Do you want a final cigarette?" I took the sock out of his mouth.

"No. You piece of ...." I put the sock back in his mouth.

"Glad you don't smoke, you'll live longer that way. I hate smokers. They are the saddest people around. Talk about addiction. The sad thing is they won't admit it. Stupid I guess."

The doctor wanted to say something. I took the sock out of his mouth. "The same can be said of you. You're stupid, an addict and a serial killer. I'm sure your mother is proud of you."

"I'm only stupid if I get caught. I do have an addiction. And I am selfish. It's not your fault. You did your best these past six weeks. I'll find a way to solve this problem. But in the meantime, it feels good."

The nice psychiatrist then passed away. I was sorry to see him go in a way. He was a nice sounding board to my thoughts and feelings. I erased my name from his weekly calendar. Oh, my name is Brianna, Bri for short, and I'm about to take you on a journey of life, death, love, sex, and my personal scoreboard of creative ways to kill.

ᏯᐤChapter TwoᐤᏉ

My First Kill

When I was thirteen years old, and in junior high school, one of my physical education teachers took his entire class to a public swimming pool. We did this once a month and we had the entire pool to ourselves. The pool was Olympic size and had five diving boards, the tallest being the ten-meter platform or about thirty feet high.

The platform diving board scared the shit out of me. But I felt I needed to conquer it. So, on our next to last trip to the pool, I went up to the top of the diving board and did …nothing. I kept looking down. I kept thinking that I wanted to jump but I kept thinking that a jump that high would do "bad things to me."

So, I stayed up there and kept looking and looking and looking down with the hopes it would look shorter or smaller or whatever. Then the bell rang, and all the other students left the pool but me. The only person around was the coach, and he didn't say a word, and me, this not-so-brave little girl on top of the diving board.

I knew my time was up. Everybody else was in the locker room. The coach was signaling me to do something, anything. Then I thought to myself. *You've come this far, you can't chicken out now.* So, I counted to ten, and I just jumped.

On the way down, my stomach seemed to leave my body as if I were on a roller coaster. But I landed, splash, no injuries. I survived. It was exhilarating. I cried. I accomplished something I hadn't accomplished before. I was so happy. The coach congratulated me. So did a couple of students who snuck out of the locker room to watch.

But here's the interesting thing. When the class came back to the pool the following month, I went directly to the ten-meter platform board and jumped off. Then I did it again, and again, and again. No problem, no sweat, no anxiety. I had it conquered.

Five years later, I had just turned eighteen, and I was a cheerleader for my college football team, the University of Oregon. I ran into a situation at a hotel in of all places Las Vegas. I left my room on the fifteenth floor of Caesar's Palace to get some ice. It was a fairly long walk from my room to the ice chest but I wanted ice for the soda I was drinking.

This man accosted me at the ice chest, introduced himself as a deacon and an alumnus of the opposing school we were playing. He was in training to eventually become a priest for the Catholic Church. He told me he needed some help back in his room unpacking his school's souvenirs his church was selling and offered me $200.00 to help him. He said with the both of us, it would only take a half hour.

Once in his room, there were several sets of souvenirs in sight but they all seemed to be evenly divided into plastic bags of all sizes. I figured he didn't need me, so I just told him so, and started to leave. He immediately jumped me, pushed me down on the bed and started to touch my breasts and pubic areas.

I said to him, "Yes, I can see you are in training to be a Catholic priest. Is this class called Rape 101?" He slapped me.

He then took off my pants and panties and was seconds away from entering me. But I was determined not to be raped so I just started kicking him. On his jaw with my bare heels, in his groin with my knees. Cheerleading practice had come in handy. Face, groin, anywhere I could connect. Enough kicks and he got off me. I started to leave but he grabbed me again, so I turned and with all the force I could manage, I kicked him in the balls. He doubled over. I found a medium size plastic bag full of souvenirs, dumped out the souvenirs and put the plastic bag over his head.

"Do you believe in God now? If so, he better do something to get you out of this plastic bag. Or Mr. Deacon, you won't make Priesthood. You sleazebag."

I just kept pulling, he just kept sucking for air and within a minute or so, he was gone. In my mind I was thinking *"Good frikken riddance,"* but I just started to cry. I had killed someone. He deserved it but he was still dead. I lost my stomach again just like when I was diving at the swimming pool. I went into the bathroom, and bowed down to the porcelain queen and barfed big time.

I sat down on the bed, stopped crying but all of a sudden this feeling of power came over me. I didn't feel so bad after all.

It was the beginning of a whole new me. I called hotel security, they took my statement, they called the police, and they took my statement. I told them that this man of God was planning on doing "bad things to me" and I had to defend myself. Our school football coach vouched for me. Our cheerleading coach vouched for me. I wasn't arrested. The deacon had evidently done this before. Twice. But never charged.

The Catholic school apologized to me privately. Offered me some money as a settlement. I told them I wouldn't take it. I went to the game the next day and cheered my ass off, Go Ducks! I cheered for our school as if nothing had happened.

I didn't kill anybody else for over four years, not until I moved to Las Vegas, and, as with diving off a platform in the swimming pool, each time it got easier and easier.

No problem, no sweat, no crying, no anxiety. I had it conquered.

Chapter Three

The Love of My Life

I almost got married and had I done so, who knows if I would have turned out the way I did. He was the love of my life, of that I am certain.

Sure, there were men I enjoyed being with these last few years that could have developed into a relationship. But I didn't let it happen.

And, of course, there were other men I dated but in all fairness to them, I didn't give them enough time to develop a relationship with me. My addiction took over. I was more interested in giving them one last glorious night to go out on and more absorbed in seeing my artistic creations come to life ...or death.

But nobody compares to Justin Prestwich, whom I grew up with, and who later became a University of Oregon Duck mascot. Justin and I went to elementary school together. We became best friends and were always on the lookout for each other's safety.

Justin and I were inseparable. Even in high school and college. We took an improv comedy class together. That's where he developed his Duck mascot humor.

We went to record stores together when they were open and listened to each other's favorite singers or rock groups. That's where I learned about Warren Zevon.

Justin had already known about him. We volunteered on four Thanksgivings together to feed the homeless at a local Portland or Eugene shelter. We shared every detail of our lives together. And here's one interesting thing we did our freshman year in college. We bought a stainless steel waterproof time capsule, took a few pictures of ourselves together, put in a piece of jewelry with both our names on it, threw in a couple more keepsakes and buried it.

The capsule was four inches in diameter, and thirteen inches tall. One night we took a walk from campus over the footbridge that crossed the Willamette River and wound up in a grassy park area just outside Autzen Stadium where the team plays its home football games. We buried it there and counted the number of paces from a given tree so we knew where it resided. We carved our initials in the tree. The Eugene City Parks and Open Spaces division still doesn't know the time capsule is there.

I learned a lot about myself sexually when we were dating, I learned how my polished and manicured bare feet could be potent. I enjoyed giving Justin a face massage with my soft soles. Every time when I did it he would wince and it would turn him on. I would slowly move my feet from his face to his chest to his groin area and back up to his face. I would circle his lips with my toes, pry open his mouth, move my toes to his tongue and then wait for him to have the urgent desire to explode.

Justin had learned a lot about my sexual interests as well. Foreplay was a big deal to me. I wanted him to touch my body in all the right spots before entering me.

He learned to be slow and deliberate. If he went through the motions, it would become apparent to me and I made him start over.

Over a period of time, we had it down to a science. We clicked. We even talked about getting married. He knew he was a good mascot and figured he could parlay that into a full time career. I still had interior design in the back of my mind but promotional modeling was not out of the question.

What I liked about Justin was he was a nice guy. Not some asshole jerk. Not some beer-drinking frat boy who couldn't grow up. I wanted a nice guy who would have a career goal in mind and would keep me safe and with food on the table and shelter above my head.

And this was the clincher. One time we were at a Portland Trail Blazers basketball game on a weekend when we were freshmen. As we were walking back to our car, two men stopped us. One guy wanted to rob Justin. The other guy wanted to move me away from the scene and I presume rape me. Justin punched the guy and ran toward the other guy to get me away from him. The guy shot Justin in the arm twice. The shots were loud so people turned around and the scumbags ran off. I took Justin to the emergency room so they could take out the bullets and patch up his arm. He was my hero that day.

Justin proposed to me in the fall of our junior year. Remember at this time, I had no deaths on my scoreboard. Not even the priest-in-training who also tried to rape me. What a proposal. I was not prepared for it. I was on the cheerleading squad for the University of Oregon and Justin, of course, was the Duck mascot on the field.

13

We won the game and after it was over Justin stopped me, got on one knee and gave me an engagement ring. The crowd was cheering. My fellow cheerleaders were crying. The scoreboard showed the event in real time.

I couldn't take off his Duck head. That was not allowed. So I opened his beak and kissed him through his Duck mouth. I'm sure it was the funniest proposal anybody had ever seen. In fact, it seems all the news shows and morning talk shows around the country showed it. We were almost famous.

How do I know Justin was the right guy for me, and how did he know I was the right girl for him. I'll take you back to the day we had The Conversation. The one that spelled things out for both of us.

"I'm not sure I'm the right guy for you," said Justin. "You could date any guy you want. You have more guys asking you out than I could ever imagine. I think half the football team wants to date you. Me, I get turned down if the girl is too beautiful. I guess I don't measure up looks wise."

"I saw a video a year or so ago," I said. "It was called The Natural Way to Meet the Right Guy. They interviewed these psychologists who said people are too picky—men and women. Each psychologist said make a list of eight qualities I wanted in a partner. Then cross out four. People are too particular. There is no such thing as a perfect partner. Justin you are the love of my life. You meet more qualities than anyone else. I don't want to date anyone but you."

"Ooh, I see, so are settling for me," he said.

I laughed. "I'm settling for the best person I have ever known in my life. I can't see myself with anybody else."

In our senior year, I was still on the cheerleading squad and Justin was still the school's Duck mascot. He was great. He got so much exposure and so many accolades pro teams wanted to hire him the minute he graduated.

My senior year was my first kill. The sleazebag priest-in-training who had tried to rape me. When he heard about it, Justin came right over and comforted me. He said all the right things. He did all the right things. But I could tell there was something different about him. His fiancé had just killed someone. A female killing another person, especially if it was justified, was a turn-on to some men. To Justin it was just the opposite.

So where did it go sideways you ask? I'm not sure to be honest.

Justin had moved to San Francisco after graduation to begin his job as a mascot with the San Francisco Giants. I was going to join him down there as soon as I finished one summer class I needed to take. Then Justin called me to tell me not to come down. He said he needed to get acclimated to his new job to see if he wanted to keep it. He said he needed to get acclimated to the Bay Area to see if he wanted to live there because housing was so expensive.

I told him I would come down and join him, do some promotional modeling and help pay the rent. He said no and would not give me a reason. I don't know if he found another girl, I don't know if he was gay, I don't know if he had some contagious disease. I just don't know what happened.

I decided to move to Las Vegas and the rest is history. I stayed in contact with Justin but calls or texts every day turned into once a week, once ever two weeks, once every month, then none at all. Here was the love of my life and we were breaking up by no choice of my own. I never found out what his reason was for calling off the engagement. But it hurt me.

If we had gotten married, I don't think I ever would have begun this killing hobby. We would be in San Francisco or some other city with a team who would hire him as its mascot. I'd probably have a kid or two by now. But things went sideways, and I'm now a pretty damn good serial killer if I do say so myself.

Chapter Four

Last 50 Cents

I had never seen a club like Last 50 Cents and I doubt if I ever will again.

Back in the 70s, there was a famous club in the notorious Roppongi District of Tokyo. It was called Last 20 Cent. No 's' after Cent. A gentleman from the United States must have traveled to Tokyo and been to this club several times because he patterned his club in Las Vegas after it. Of course, inflation and a new decade upped the ante to Last 50 Cents. Cents now plural. This club was not in a hotel. It was situated on a side street not too far from the stadium where the Las Vegas Raiders play.

Usually clubs outside Strip hotels don't make it. The walk-in traffic is not there. Last 50 Cents was different. It was packed every night with good-looking men and women, and the owner didn't even need to hire a dozen "atmosphere" girls to hang around and pretend they were interested in guys when all they were really interested in was trying to get the guys to spend more money, which they would get a cut of.

When you walk into Last 50 Cents, you first see a coat check station. A female model with blonde hair and fairly big boobs is there to greet you. You turn in your jacket, purse, or whatever you need to, and your shoes.

Yes, everybody leaves their shoes at this point. Everybody who goes in either is barefooted or has socks or hosiery on.

You then walk down a carpeted hallway, maybe thirty feet long. There you are greeted by two security people, one male, one female, who frisk you to make sure you don't have any weapons or drugs. Once frisked, you come to an iron door three feet, eleven inches high.

Since it's under four-feet tall, you can't walk straight through. You must stoop or bend to get through. Only a dwarf might be able to walk through without bending down.

Above the door is a black sign with white lettering: "To Pass Through This Door, We All Must Bend."

I loved that. Everybody equal. No guys at the door telling you who gets in and who doesn't. At the usual clubs, guys guard the rope, letting in the good-looking women, and the guys who most likely will spend the most money.

So, you would figure that Last 50 Cents would be overloaded with ugly looking fat people. But it wasn't. You had your share of average looking people but it still managed to get the best-looking men and women in town, even better than the high priced clubs in Strip hotels.

Once inside, there were no tables for two or four people. This was a surprise. The tables were round, close to the ground and could seat ten. The person who designed these tables must have studied sociology. When you have a table for two, you are stuck with the other person at that table. When you have a table for 10 you automatically get to know, even for only a minute, the other people at the table.

On one side of the club was a sunken dance floor. You take three or four steps down and you are ready to dance. On the other side was a sunken bar. This was classy. No bar stools. You just sat on a pillow on the floor and you were perfect height to the bar.

My girlfriend Kerrie and I sat down at one of those tables for ten. The pillows were very comfortable and gave your booty plenty of room to maneuver. The carpeting was very soft, comforting to your bare feet. In total there were six men at my table and four women.

One of the men asked my girlfriend if he could change places with her. He was interested in me, and his buddy was interested in Kerrie. The guy's name was Troy or Trey or something like that. He was mid 20s. Thought he was cool. Thought I was his for the taking. I let him think that way. If you want to keep a guy interested in you, I'll tell you in one sentence how it's done. "They stare at me while I stare at you." In other words, I let all the guys in the room stare at me, admire me, and wish they could be with me. If I'm interested in someone, he is the only person in the room to me. He has my undivided attention even if his eyes stray to other women.

He asked me what I did for a living, I told him that I am a promotional model, and I get plenty of work in Las Vegas because there's a convention or trade show almost every week in town. I told him all I do is just stand around and hand out brochures or introduce one of the sales guys to the people who show up at my booth. A decent looking model can make a good living in this city.

I asked him what he did for a living. He told me he was a writer and that he was here on a week's vacation from Connecticut. I thought at first that maybe he was a television writer, or maybe a screenwriter with some credits of films that actually had been made, or even an advertising copywriter. Nope, guess again. He wrote for one of the professional wrestling circuits.

"All that bravado you see and hear on TV. Yep that's me."

Yep, he was the guy who put the words into the bad guys' mouths. He helped create the conflict between the hero and the heel, as he explained it. He had been doing that for five years now and they paid him pretty handsomely to create that scintillating dialogue.

"I could take you home, pin you to the bed and show you how a champion does it." I paused, did not respond. "OK, how about this," he said. "One fall to a finish. Loser leaves town and must shave his or her legs." He was beginning to sound like one of his scripts, Boring.

"Final offer. If I make you submit to me, you give me a blow job. If you make me submit to you, I give you $500."

Now, that was tempting. "Let me see the $500 first." He pulled out his wallet, showed me he had that kind of money with him. So, I took him home, and took the $500 to hold.

Now, don't get the idea I'm a prostitute or an escort and take money for sex. I don't. I've never done it before. But this was a challenge, and I'm always up for challenges. We were on the bed, kissing. No real wrestling. Just kind of fun stuff.

Then I asked him to jump into my bathtub. "If we are going to get real sweaty wrestling or having sex, I want you clean and fresh," I said.

"OK, if you insist." He figured it was a small price to pay for a night of sexual fun. So, he jumped out of bed, and walked naked into the bathtub and turned on the water to suit his taste.

Now, the fun would begin. At least the fun for me. I walked over to the tub, kneeled down beside it and pressed a button. Chomp. I had a plastic dome installed over the tub that came down and encased the tub. I would use it once in a while to keep out the noise so I could just relax. But I had a remote with me at all times, so I could control it from the inside. This would be the first time I would use it for fun. Well, for deadly fun to be exact. I could lock it from the outside, and I did just that.

Wow, did Troy's eyes open wide. He was stunned to see himself trapped within the confines of my water dome. Then he laughed.

"OK, good one. You've got me trapped. You made me submit to you. You get to keep the $500."

But the money meant nothing now. This was a one-on-one battle to the death. He did what I expected. The water was rising, so he turned it off. I upped him one. I could control the water from the outside, and lock it so it couldn't be turned off. The water kept rising.

He started shaking and hitting the dome. That wouldn't work. It was pretty tightly made. Now, he started to worry. "You won, now please let me out of here."

"Do you believe in God?"

"What?" he said. "Why?"

"Do you believe in God?" I asked again.

"Yes, of course."

"Well, if you believe in a God, he or she better do something to get you out of there."

"Are you the devil? That's what you sound like."

"I don't believe in supreme beings or devils. That's all fiction to me."

He kept fighting, trying to break the unbreakable dome. The water level in the tub kept rising. He didn't last much longer. I left the room for fifteen minutes, made a mark on my personal scoreboard which sits behind my bed, and enjoyed the conquest.

Chapter Five

Poof ...And Now He's Gone

About 129 miles south of Las Vegas off the 15 freeway, is a somewhat famous torn-down amusement park called Rock-A-Hoola Water Park. You've probably never heard of it.

It was built in the early 60s and closed in 2004. It consisted of steel slides, a man-made lake, and a popular lazy river people could swim in, plus all the usual concessions.

At one point even though it was not near anything, it developed a solid reputation, and became a popular tourist destination. Then in 1999 one employee took a late night water ride into a pool that was only slightly filled. The employee's landing did not go well and he became a paraplegic. A legal settlement cost the waterpark millions of dollars and Rock-A-Hoola was never able to fully recover. Five years later, it was totally shut down.

Now, vandals and scavengers have damaged most of the buildings and signs. For me this is good. Why? Because this is where I put these lost souls I've eliminated. I needed a place to get rid of them that was far enough away so people wouldn't get too concerned. After all, most of them were from out of town.

On this day I gathered up Troy, placed him in my trunk and took off. Actually late in the day approaching dusk is when I try to head out. Usually the graffiti artists show up in the middle of the night and leave the place alone in the early evening.

I drive the speed limit, never speed. The last thing I need is for a cop to stop me. First I pass Primm, the border between California and Nevada. The highlight of this area is The Lottery Store, located on the California side of the border. Since Nevada does not have a lottery, thanks mostly to the lobbyists from the casino industry, people from Las Vegas drive to The Lottery Store to buy lottery tickets for California's lotteries. The place is always crowded, and if the Lottery winnings total is really large, you can be waiting in line for two hours before you get your tickets. I usually stop at the store to buy one ticket. It makes me feel good to buy a ticket. It makes me feel like I have a chance at winning millions, even though I've never won more than $100.

Then I'm off to Rock-A-Hoola. First I pass Halloran Summer Road, home to an isolated pink house, some nice looking Joshua Trees, and reportedly a few dead bodies of famous mafia associates from the old Vegas days. Next landmark is Baker, home to the World's Tallest Thermometer standing at 134-feet high. Then I pass Zzyzx Rd before coming upon the Newbury Springs area. I turn off at Harvard Road, and then turn onto Hacienda Rd.

I pass Saint Antony's Monastery, which looks like a trailer park, and finally come upon Rock-A-Hoola Water Park where everything is abandoned. This is where the resting place of many of my dates wind up.

I bring along a motorized shovel and find an empty area at the bottom of one of the steel slides. This area is not cement any longer. It has long ago been dug up. It's now mostly dirt. I check to see if anybody is around, and then start digging. The motorized shovel digs holes faster and deeper than a normal shovel. Sure, I can pay somebody to help me. But I won't. I want to be the only person to know the whereabouts of my victims. Once you tell a second person, you're done. That person will eventually try and blackmail you and then report you to the police. Telling a second person is like telling a newspaper reporter. Pretty soon word gets out to everybody.

If my count is correct, I've buried eight or nine up and down the section that was once the lazy river. No water is running down this "river," which used to run on artificial current, and people would swim it. Today, it's part cement, and part loose dirt, so not too difficult to dig up.

I finished my digging, said my good-byes to Troy, and headed home. I stop at The Lottery Store once again, grab a Diet Pepsi, now without Aspartame, and purchase one more Mega Millions lottery ticket. I'm sure I'll win this time.

I leave The Lottery Store and get into a line of cars waiting to enter the freeway. It's a small on-ramp, so only one car at a time jumps in. I'm second in line when all of a sudden an old souped up Chevy driven by a teenager speeds in front of the line and enters the on-ramp. The car cuts off the first car in line, hits it in the front, and spins it around, forcing it to go off the highway and roll over. The teen driver speeds away. I immediately get out of my Lexus as does the gentleman who has the Toyota Corolla right behind me, and we rush over to the car that had just turned over.

Inside was a woman and her young child, maybe six or seven years old, and we both help free them from their seatbelts and pull them to safety.

We stayed with them for about fifteen or twenty minutes until they both regained consciousness. I start to get back into my car. The man with the Toyota said, "You're a hero. You should at least let the cops get your name to give to the newspapers and TV stations." I thank him, and tell him I need to get back into town. I wish him and the injured woman, and the little girl well, and get in my car and drive away.

Given my past experience, I can't take the chance the local cops would want to talk to me. Maybe I'm a hero or maybe not but it's not important to me that anybody knows.

#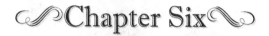

The Telephone Club

Talk about one of the most unique clubs ever created. Welcome to Ring, Ring, often referred to simply as the Telephone Club. It was patterned after a club in Berlin that was popular in the 50s, 60s and 70s called Club Rezi. Club Rezi was a large nightclub with a live band and a large dance floor. No bullshit DJs spinning crap with people jumping up and down waving large light bulbs. You would sit at individual tables that had an elaborate system of table phones and pneumatic tubes. This allowed for anonymous late night flirtation between complete strangers.

Club Rezi opened in 1908 and closed in 1939 before World War II. It re-opened in 1951 and closed for good in 1978. The Chicago Tribune wrote an article on it, and it became popular with Americans who were visiting Berlin.

According to the Berlin Herald, "the tabletop telephones buzzed, and before you knew it, the blonde, raven haired or redheaded monocle-wearing beauty had an invite to dance. She was no longer alone."

For those too shy to pick up the phone, the pneumatic tubes offered a perfect alternative. The tubes were built into the handrails, and one was located at each table. The nightclub provided paper on which to scrawl notes. Patrons only had to specify where they wanted their notes sent. Table number thirty-five, Table number fifty-five. This was today's answer to text messaging, I guess. The Berlin newspaper continued, "Many provocative notes were passed around but eager flirters still needed to be careful. Messages sent by the tube were checked by female 'censors' in the switchboard room.

This table mail service was real, and allowed patrons to send more than just a handwritten note to that stranger across the way.

The Rezi offered a long menu of gifts that visitors could dispatch via pneumatic tube—including perfume bottles, cigar cutters, travel plans and, according to one source, cocaine.

In Las Vegas, the security was tight. I had never heard of any cocaine problems at Ring, Ring. We paid a twenty dollar cover.

Everybody—male or female—paid the same cover. And one thing I was appreciative of, you weren't forced to buy a twenty dollar bottle of vodka for $500. Normal drinks, normal drink prices.

I took at seat with my friend Kerrie, and we waited to see if we had any suitors. But this was a unique night. This was costume night. They do this once a month. Many people were dressed in costume. Of course, over half were super heroes. Kerrie liked the Superhero type. I was looking for someone with a little more imagination.

I liked the guy in a chef's outfit with dozens of cereal boxes stapled to his outfit and fake blood running down his clothes. A man after my own heart, a Cereal Killer. But he was not to be. He smiled at me, I smiled back, but I could see he was already taken at another table.

Then I saw this guy dressed in all black. Black t-shirt, showing off his muscles. Black jeans. Black mask that just went over his eyes. And he was carrying three' plastic baseball bats. It took me a minute. But Batman was my new hero. I could see he had already joined another table with another girl.

Kerrie had found her Spiderman. But I was still solo on this trip. Then all of a sudden, right before me was this clown. This was actually a nice-looking clown. Nice smile. Nice teeth. Nice jaw.

"Where have all the scary-looking clowns gone?" I asked him.

He introduced himself as Bruce or Bob or something that started with a B. I told him I would just call him Bozo. Bozo had a delightful demeanor at first. We talked politics, feature films, economics, sexual positions. I asked him if he wanted to go back to my place and of course, he accepted.

Bozo liked to get rough. He pushed me down on my king-size Casper bed and got on top of me. He started slapping me on the cheek, first lightly, then harder. Certainly not becoming of a peaceful clown.

I knew some wrestling from my high school days, so I scissored his head and took him down by swinging my legs to the side. I then moved my scissors around one of his arms, trapping it. He couldn't move it. I held his other arm immobile. For you wrestling aficionados, this is called a Crucifix.

I then put my finger to his mouth, slowly circling his lips and then his tongue. He enjoyed that. Then I put the sharp beautifully polished pink nails of my thumb and forefinger and pinched hard. His tongue started to bleed. He tried to hit me but my crucifix hold kept him in check. I could see that behind that clown makeup he was pissed.

"Hey, Bozo, do you believe in God?"

"Yeah, I do and if I don't punish you first, he will."

"Why did you dress as a clown tonight?"

"I always dress as a clown. It puts some joy in people's lives and if you are a nice clown I have a better chance of taking women home."

"You got me home all right, Bozo, but what if I told you, that I had put some poison on these two fingernails and it was now running around your bloodstream."

He began fighting harder. "I'm going to kick your ass."

"You'll be dead before that. Unless that God of yours saves you, you'll be my first clown kill."

His breathing was labored, and I finished him off by closing off air passages over his mouth and nose. I let him sleep in my room and took a drive the next evening to Rock-A-Hoola Water Park. Turned on some Warren Zevon.

"There's his red nose on the ground.

No one's seen his painted smile.

Something bad happened to a clown."

I stopped once again at The Lottery Store, bought a large diet Pepsi without aspartame, and two lottery tickets. But once again I didn't win.

Chapter Seven

MET A MAN, WENT TO THE TURKS AND CAICOS, DIDN'T KILL HIM.

I've always been a Warren Zevon fan. He was a great singer/songwriter who died too young back in 2004. Warren Zevon was the best songwriter I knew of. He would tell a story. Usually with a start, middle and end. Journalists and writers admired him.

Most singers/songwriters write some poetic excuse the expression bullshit. It's mostly about love—either gaining it or losing it—but it never seems authentic. It seems faked. The emotional attachment is not there. I never believe the singer is/was really in love. I think they are filling up the song with words but they don't mean a thing. Kind of like, going through the motions.

Mr. Zevon always had a way with words. It's what made him who he was. It could be a gimmick song such as Werewolves of London or Hit Somebody, better known as The Hockey Song, or it could be something more poetic such as Desperadoes under the Eaves or Mutineer. Whatever, he always had a great story to tell.

I love to donate to charity events. For this one I paid $100. It was a group of fairly famous performers such as Jackson Browne and Dawes and they were doing a two-hour show of Warren Zevon material to benefit a battered women's shelter. I went to the post-concert party and met a guy. His name was Tom. We got along well, mainly due to the fact that we both had Zevon's music in common. After going out five times, he wanted to take me to the Turks and Caicos, one of those tourist islands just down the block from the Bahamas. I enjoyed his company, the kissing was good, the protected sex was good, so I agreed.

We stayed at a nice resort with the biggest most gorgeous swimming pool I've ever seen. Our room had a nice ocean view and a comfortable king-size bed. Tom booked a sweet deal for us. Pay for four days and get the fifth one free.

I remember two specific things about our time in the Turks and Caicos. First, every Thursday night everybody who was anybody would go to the Island Fish Fry. This was basically local food vendors, including some of the top restaurants on the island, getting together every week to sell their dinners. Some people were selling out of their food trucks. Other restaurants had set up an area where they would cook their best dishes.

The best restaurants, of course, had the longest lines, so that's where we gravitated to. This fish fry happened to be situated on a large empty lot right next to the hotel we were at, so it was convenient for us. At the end of the food area was a stage where some of the local musical talent would present a concert. We enjoyed it very much, and went back to the hotel and relished our romantic time in bed together.

The other specific thing I remember almost got me killed or at the very least kidnapped. It was one of the few times I was actually scared of dying. Now, I felt like some of my former dates did, knowing this could be the end.

Tom wanted to swim in the pool. I wanted to do some island shopping. He gave me $100 and I had the hotel drop me off at a small outdoor shopping mall. I spent about ninety minutes shopping, buying only a bathing suit.

In the Turks and Caicos, you don't call a cab. You just wait for one to drive by. I must have waited for a half-hour at this mall, and no taxi came by. This older lady, whom I believe was Haitian, told me to be patient and a taxi would be coming in a few minutes. Sure, enough a taxi came by and I told him the name of my hotel. The woman said she was going in the same direction and without even asking she jumped in. Twenty minutes later we were still driving. I knew we weren't going in the same direction as my hotel, so I made a comment to the driver. The Haitian woman assured me she would get me back to my hotel. But I had a feeling I was being kidnapped. I had a feeling I was about to become a victim of sex trafficking. They were going to take me to some boat landing and put me on a boat to who-knows-where and nobody would ever hear from me again.

I started to get angry and I demanded the taxi driver let me out of the cab now. The lady slapped me and told me to shut up. Then all of a sudden things changed. The lady asked me what I was doing in the Turks and Caicos. I told her my fiancé and I had just got engaged and this was my fiancé's treat. She asked me what my fiancé did for a living, and I told her he was a police detective in Los Angeles. That seemed to do the trick. She told the cab driver to pull over and stop the car. They let me go. I walked about a half-mile to a hotel, called Tom and told him what happened.

He asked the shuttle from our hotel to drive to where I was located. He got out of the shuttle, ran over to me, kissed me like I've never been kissed before, and we went back to our hotel. We left the Turks and Caicos the next day. I was alive and so was he.

I was hoping to continue my relationship with Tom but over the next six months we slowly drifted apart and he stopped calling me. I figured he found another Warren Zevon lover.

Chapter Eight

THE CAREER I ALMOST WANTED

For about ten minutes I wanted to be an interior designer. When I moved to Las Vegas, I signed up for a ten-week course. If I liked it, I was going to continue with the advanced courses. The one thing I liked about it was they weren't trying to force any style of design on you. The final say is, of course, up to the client. But If I have a specific taste, I am allowed to pursue it and promote it. So, after taking both courses, I decided to call myself an interior designer. I had business cards made and a website built with photos of living rooms, dens and bedrooms I created while in class. My first client was a rich bachelor, Cort Smith, a handsome guy in his early thirties. His taste of high tech and my taste of contemporary pretty much coincided. He had a big living room. I asked him one question. "Did he entertain?" When he told me yes, I immediately thought of Masanori Umeda's Memphis Milano Conversation Pit. Basically, it was a big couch that looked like a wrestling ring in which people could sit anywhere. Each corner had a pillow. The center had a pillow. You were always facing somebody, making contact with somebody.

The wrestling ring couch was very comfortable. It was even surrounded by fluffy ropes you had to climb through to get "inside" the couch. This was not a cheap piece of furniture, $50,000 would cover it.

When it was delivered, it kind of turned me on. I love mixing it up with men. A little bit of wrestling is, to put it bluntly, sexual. At this point in time, I hadn't even thought of being a serial killer. Cort asked me if I wanted to launch it. I didn't hesitate and we both stepped inside the "ring" for a little playful wrestling.

I could have killed Cort, but my mind wasn't thinking along those lines yet, although it was getting closer. I remember when I was thirteen years old and was hiking a couple of miles from my parents' house near Portland. I came across a couple of teens, maybe high school age, maybe even college age. They were making love—out and out sexual intercourse and I had never seen that before. Seriously, I never even watched porno films. They were kissing, rolling, and touching and it turned me on. It was the first time I could remember when I felt a sexual feeling in my body.

After about fifteen minutes of rolling around, the girl put a piece of chocolate in her boyfriend's mouth. He swallowed the candy, kissed her one more time, and laid down peacefully and died. She tried to shake him to wake up. He never did. I don't know if she purposely killed him or it was an accident but nevertheless, he was dead. The girl was crying but she was calm. She did not scream. She kissed him on the cheek, put on her clothes and walked away. I stayed there another fifteen minutes to see if the girl would come back. She did not. I slowly tip toed over to the body and noticed he had a smile on his face.

This was a coming of age moment for me. I saw a dead body for the first time, a body whose death was caused by a young female either purposely or inadvertently. This was death in person and, I'm being honest here, it caused me to experience my first orgasm. My first of many.

I was doing well professionally as an interior designer until I met Mrs. Brenda Rothstein. Mrs. Rothstein, in her early thirties, was the wife of jeans magnate Stuart Rothstein. She was beautiful but she was a prima donna to be sure. Brenda was someone who had never worked a day in her life. She grew up wealthy and married into more wealth. And her word was final. Whatever she wanted was final.

I didn't have a problem with Brenda's ultimate goal of being the final decision maker because in her own words she was "The Goddess of Interior Design." Who's to argue with that self-imposed title? But I did have a problem with the fact she couldn't make up her mind.

With a live-in maid, a gardener three days a week, and a live-in chef, Brenda had plenty of time to play "goddess." I could live with Brenda if she were only nitpicky. But it seems she spent every waking moment complaining.

I had a feeling she would be a pain to work with so I charged her hourly instead of a flat rate. She would pick out furniture, we would order it, it would be delivered, and she would hate it. This happened four times. I tried to tell her what would look good in her house but she would have none of it. She kept telling me, she knew what was best for her own mansion.

Most clients were a pleasure to work with. They allowed me to suggest things, they either approved or disapproved, we took one or two shopping trips together and we were done. Mrs. Rothstein seemed to complain for the sake of complaining. It was frustrating to deal with her. Finally, after sparring with her for five weeks, and getting nowhere, I gave up.

"Mrs. Rothstein, am I your first interior designer on this project?" I asked.

"No, you are my third."

"Do you think the other two left you because you couldn't make up your mind?"

"I fired both of them. I didn't like their taste."

"Well, I'm done here. All we do is spar and argue, and it's disheartening. You can't make up your mind even after going to a furniture store and choosing what you want."

"All the best to you and your next choice of interior designer. But I've had enough. I'm going to send you an invoice and if it's not paid, I will take you to court."

She complained that I was not a good interior designer and not professional enough for her. I said that was her opinion. But I'm still leaving. And that was it, I decided the interior design business was not for me. I took a few more gigs but I didn't like answering to people who couldn't make up their minds. That was when I decided to become a promotional model. I could set my own hours, work when I wanted to, and I didn't have to answer to anybody. And maybe I could begin my hobby of killing.

↞Chapter Nine↠

THE KING AND HIS OLD FARTS

There's a guy in Las Vegas who refers to himself as The King.

Talk about a fool. He throws a party every three or four months in the name of high-end networking but also because he and his ego love it when people pay homage to him. He rents out a suite at one of the Strip hotels and invites fifty to one hundred people.

He wears a bright red king's robe, which probably came from some Halloween costume store. It's more like a cape and ties around the neck. The shoulders have a distinct leopard pattern to them. And, of course, a cheap crown comes with it. The crown had been known to fall off a dozen times every party so he finally had the smarts to pin it down to his big head.

His guests come from mostly the gaming world but he sprinkles in some entertainers and a few other mildly un-important people. Sometimes he has some of these people get up and tell what they do for a living. People mingle and make business contacts and a good time is had by all. Then he waits for the guests to say thank you to him, either when they speak in front of the rest of the group or after the event is over.

He's one of those guys who won't let you forget there is a God somewhere running around saving you. He's a religious zealot, although he doesn't preach it as I was told he used to.

Many of these people are his friends, many are his clients. He supplements that group with some so-called performers and celebrities. The celebrities are has-beens. They were famous actresses from the 80s, famous singers from the 70s, famous actors from shows that ran in the late 70s. It would be a shock to see if he invited (and they accepted) a current name actor or performer. It's not that they are forgotten now, or that they lack talent. It's just that no one cares about them any longer, so they attend the King's party to get one last round of applause. Then The King sprinkles in some performers. We have a minor league Blues Brothers tribute duo that sings a couple of songs and throws out souvenir sweat socks to the crowd. We have a Madonna tribute artist who looks older than the real Madonna. We have an almost-famous singer who once performed in a "bubble gum" pop group in the 70s. In short, we have a lot of old farts and a lot of second-rate talent.

I have attended three of The King's events. I was hired by a modeling agency to serve food and drinks, and I thought it would be an interesting change from a convention or trade show.

One thing I learned about Las Vegas models. They don't show up to a party even if invited unless they are paid to attend. I was getting paid, so I thought *"Why Not?"* I didn't mind that I didn't see anyone in their twenties. I like to date older guys. The guys I like to kill are much younger.

Younger guys don't know how to date. They want to take you to a club and drink. Nothing intimate about it. These guys think I'll be impressed when they pay $425 for a bottle of Ketel One vodka instead of the usual $500 and then they tell me they got a discount because they know the club's general manager personally. Stupid kids. I was serving a drink to this guy in his early fifties. Ray or Ralph, or something like that. Executive vice president of a major gaming company whose main form of income was to license a well-known television game show and put it on a slot machine. This kind of marketing is good for the television show, and good for the bottom line of the hotels that place them in strategic spots, and good for the gaming companies that sell them. I thought he was an attractive man, so I agreed to go out for a drink with him after The King's event had closed down.

We hit it off pretty well. I told him I thought it was a good event with a lot of old farts. He laughed and agreed, even though he was one of the old farts I was referring to.

Ray could talk and talk. He would go from one topic of conversation directly to another. He actually became pretty annoying.

I barely got a word in. Travel, politics, one of the performers who sang tonight and eventually he would end up talking about slot machines. He had a "disease" I call TMD. Too Much Detail. If he was giving someone an address of a restaurant, he would go over every stop sign, every right turn, and then name the top ten things from their menu. That's a guy with TMD.

He told me he owns seven antique slot machines, all of which work.

41

When he throws a party, he usually has enough people playing his slots to make up most of the cost of his party. He thought I would be impressed with his knowledge of slot machines so, of course, he was going to tell me all he knew.

A variation of the slot machine was invented by two guys from Brooklyn in 1891. Then a few years later, a gentleman from San Francisco revised it to something close to what is seen today. In those days, sometimes your winnings came in the form of fruit-flavored chewing gum.

Bally took it up a notch in 1963 according to Ray. Its slot machine, known as Money Honey, became the first to offer an automatic payout of up to 500 coins without the help of an attendant. A whole new world was born to older Midwesterners who would come to Vegas to smoke, drink and gamble away their paychecks.

I took Ray home, threw him down on the bed, and before he knew it, I had tied his wrists to the bedposts. I excused myself, put on my pink gloves, put some special super glue on the fingers of my gloves, and waited for him to try and open a discussion about another topic.

Sure, enough, he started waxing poetic about Bondage and Discipline. Before he had a chance to get deep into it, I asked him about God.

"Do you believe in a God?" I asked.

"Definitely."

"How do you know there's a God?"

"He helps me make decisions."

"You mean, you make the decision, and give the credit to this God of yours."

"No. I believe I am talking to the real God."

"That's gibberish."

Before he had a chance to get further into it, I rubbed the Super-Glued glove fingers across his lips. The softness of my strokes turned him on.

"Ray, if there is a God out there, it needs to hurry up and save you from a serial killer like myself."

He tried opening his mouth to talk. He couldn't. His lips were stuck together. I'm sure he figured his professional gift of gab would save him. Nope, not a chance. I kissed him on the cheek, covered his nose so he couldn't breathe and he passed away peacefully. The gaming industry had just lost another highly capable slot machine executive vice president.

The next day I drove to Rock-A-Hoola Water Park and buried him. On the way back to Las Vegas, I stopped once again at The Lottery Store, bought a diet Pepsi without aspartame and three Mega Millions tickets and drove home. I was certain one of these tickets was a winner. Probably not. But it gave me something to look forward to.

ᴄᴗᴖChapter Tenᴖᴗᴐ

Clean Up On Section Nine

For the first time in my life, I decided to watch the Lottery Show. For some reason, I had a strong feeling I was going to win something. Even if it were only a few bucks.

In the next few minutes, my entire life changed. I watched as the ping-pong balls popped out of the machine. I had that one, and that one, and that makes three. Number four was also mine. Didn't connect on the fifth number. But I hit on the sixth. I was a winner. Maybe not the grand prize but a big prize nonetheless. As I learned the next morning. I had won $510, 444. Hooray for me. I was rich, or at least richer than I was yesterday. So, my first thought was how will these new riches change my life? I decided I would give some of it away to a charity to be determined later. But I would not give up my life as a serial killer. Demented as that may seem, I enjoyed it too much.

I had just heard on the local news that they had found a dead body of a guy dressed as a clown at Rock-A-Hoola. I sure hoped I hadn't left any DNA behind. But I wasn't going to worry about it now.

Why worry twice is my motto. If they have found something, then I can react. If not, I go on with my business. I'm usually pretty careful about these things. I wear gloves when I do my burying.

My next date and possible kill was in an unusual place. IKEA. I really hated IKEA. I hated it because you had to walk through a maze to get where you wanted to go, and if you bought something of any substance, you had to spend hours putting it together.

I went to a seafood restaurant one night. It was called Jakes, and the waiter told me I had invented a new seafood term. I called it The IKEA Lobster. This is a lobster they swear is easy to crack and eat. But when you get it served to you it's impossible to open, let alone enjoy, much like a piece of IKEA furniture that takes hours to put together. The first time I went to this restaurant it took three people from the serving staff to attempt to open the lobster and they all failed. Finally, the Oyster shucker figured out how to open it.

When you go to IKEA, they swear to you that any given piece of furniture can be easily put together. But as you find out, it's not that easy. Some of the directions are just wrong. Sometimes they don't give you the correct, necessary tools. I bought a bedroom cabinet. I figured I'm resourceful, so I would attempt to put it together myself. After one hour and fifty-three minutes of unnecessary stress, I called IKEA and they sent over a guy a day later to finish putting it together. They still charged me $100.

I'm just getting started. The bedroom cabinet I wanted was in section nine. So I started at section one and then figured I would make the necessary twists and turns to get to section nine. But then I saw a shortcut, or what I thought was a shortcut. A sign pointed me to a shortcut to section eight. So I get to section eight, and then figured it would be easy to find section nine. Only there wasn't a section nine.

You jump from section eight to section ten. The sign that points to section nine actually takes you to an emergency exit.

So I asked two IKEA saleswomen to get me to section nine and I even offered them ten dollars each to take me there. They both declined, saying they didn't know where section nine was. They both pointed in the direction that I started to follow earlier but I told them I did that and it didn't take me to nine. I then backtracked back to the original route with no shortcuts and eventually found section nine. I ordered what I needed, paid for it and drove back home.

But I wanted to show IKEA a lesson. I wanted to see if the cops could get to section nine without any problem. I set up my next date at IKEA. His name was Steve or Stuart or something like that. I told him I wanted to do something a little different, make love in a public place. I told him I would meet him at the entrance to IKEA, a half-hour before closing time.

When he showed up, I gave him a five-minute head start and told him to meet me in section nine. I took the regular route. As I expected, he followed the shortcut to section eight and got lost. Eventually, he found me in section nine. I had picked out a bed for us and made sure it was hidden from view by putting some cabinets and chests of drawers in front of it.

Stuart told me he was a local commercial producer, but he recently finished a charity production for Make A Wish Foundation in which a seven-year-old boy with cancer wanted his wish to be Spiderman fulfilled. He didn't want to meet Spiderman, he wanted to be Spiderman.

Stuart got the fire department to let the little boy, dressed in a Spiderman outfit, climb a hook and ladder up the side of the Westgate Hotel.

One thing led to another and we wound up in the Elvis Suite, which, of course, was the suite Elvis used to sleep in and change clothes in before he went on stage. This was when the Westgate had earlier been the Las Vegas Hilton. Rumor has it Elvis accidentally shot a pistol in the suite, thereby creating a bullet hole with the bullet still lodged in the wall. But if this was true, nobody could find either the bullet or bullet hole.

Spiderman needed a bad guy, of course, so comedian Carrot Top filled that role beautifully. Carrot Top had tied up three Elvis impersonators, and Spiderman was there to save the day. Using his trusty weapon that shot out silly string, Spiderman managed to capture Carrot Top. I loved the story.

I was enjoying my date. So what could go wrong? I had no immediate plans to end Stuart's life. We enjoyed our time under the covers in bed, and no one from IKEA found us. Section nine was hidden well, from even security. But I still wanted to show IKEA a lesson, so I cut off Stuart's airways with a sleeper hold, tied him up with his hands against a bedpost and his ankles against the opposite bedpost, and put a gag in his mouth.

He would wake up fairly soon but he would have a tough time going anywhere and an even tougher time explaining how he got into that position. He was pretty much stuck. I left the store out an employee's entrance with no one the wiser. I'm not sure when they found him because I never heard from Stuart again. But I decided to donate $100,000 out of my recent lottery winnings to Make A Wish Foundation. I felt good about that.

Chapter Eleven

The Dating Game

I'm going to admit it now. I haven't had many boyfriends. I'm too picky. And if I find someone I really like, I usually do something to end the relationship. I subconsciously sabotage it. Or I just kill the guy.

My last boyfriend was Arthur. We went out for three years. That's a new world record for me. I liked him a lot. He liked to go to the theatre, so did I. He liked concerts, so did I. He liked sports, so did I. He came up with these satirical comments that I loved. I would accidentally put my hand on his crotch when we were watching Netflix, which he loved.

But I came to the conclusion I'm a loner. I enjoy doing things by myself. I enjoy going to movies alone. I sometimes travel alone. I've even gone to sports events by myself. I guess if you are a serial killer you don't want too many friends. I try to have friends but I don't want them getting too close to me.

I met Arthur at SeekingSugarDaddy.com. I had heard about this from my friend Kerrie. She said she had met some decent guys from the site and they would always pay her something to go out even just for dinner, and you weren't required to have sex unless you wanted to.

Arthur was an older guy about to turn sixty. He was a nice-looking man, with a nice disposition. He was smart, opinionated, not religious, so we seemed to click. He also had a foot fetish. He had a difficult time having normal sexual intercourse because he would go soft once inside me, or any woman. But if I put my bare feet in his face, he would stay hard.

We would usually go out to a concert or a Vegas show and then we would head back to his high-rise condo adjacent to the Strip and go directly to his bedroom. He would always ask me to wash my feet before getting into his bed. Once in bed, he would ejaculate quickly. I would alternate kissing him and putting my feet in his face. He would get hard within a few minutes. Then I would either jack him off or he would do it himself. He was an explosive boy, that's for sure. Some guys dribble it out. He shot it out.

After his explosion, we would lay next to each other kissing for a few minutes, and then he would give me $500 and I'd be on my way. We would see each other once a week. I never asked for $500. I really didn't ask for any money. A nice dinner, or concert or show would be sufficient for me. But that's the way the game was played on this Seeking Sugar Daddy website. A man was expected to pay something to the female date. I'm sure a lot of women paid all their monthly bills from this website.

We dated for three years, certainly enough time for me to figure out if I was in love with him. When it wouldn't interfere with my side passion of dating—okay, killing—other men, we would take side trips. San Francisco, San Diego, New York for Broadway shows, even Cleveland because we were both interested in seeing The Rock and Roll Hall of Fame. We took one two-week trip to Europe—Venice, Barcelona, London and Edinburgh.

He almost dumped me for good after our trip to Venice. I kept wanting to go shopping. He wanted to see the sights. In Venice, street addresses are pretty worthless. You start at St. Mark's Square, pick a street and just go from one store to another. He hated it. Finally, I agreed to go with him on a romantic gondola ride. I think that saved our relationship.

I have to admit the gondola ride was pretty interesting. Our tour guide told us that at one time over 100,000 residents lived in Venice proper. Now only 55,000 live there full time. You can see by the closed apartments that the city had taken a turn for the worse. But Venice still prospers if it doesn't get flooded. It is said that over 50,000 tourists arrive and leave the same day. They all come from luxury cruise liners that dock on the outskirts of Venice and they all take boat rides to Venice proper where they spend money like there is no tomorrow. The retail store workers live on outlying islands and show up, go to work, and go home at closing time.

Barcelona was enjoyable for both of us, especially Park Guell and anything else having to do with the architecture of Gaudi. London was ok, especially The Tower of London, and we both thought Edinburgh was one of the most beautiful cities in Europe. Our hotel room had a view of Edinburgh Castle.

I ended the relationship when he told me he had met another girl on the Sugar Daddy site and he had gotten her pregnant. He was going to marry her and support the kid. I was surprised, but I wished him well.

I really enjoyed my three years with Arthur and there was no way I would consider ending his life but at the same time I didn't want to get married to him either, and I told him I was happy for him that he found a woman he could connect with. He was the first and last Sugar Daddy I dated for any length of time.

ⳣChapter Twelveⳤ

Yes, I Do Have an Opinion About You

OK, I'll be the first to admit, I am judgmental. I have opinions about things—people, places, events, and I'm not afraid to speak out on them.

Take art for example. Some people love Van Gogh, Rembrandt, Monet, Picasso, Dali, Warhol, Lichtenstein, even those dogs that play poker. All that is just a personal preference, a matter of taste. Can't fault a person who has good taste or even bad taste. As long as they have an opinion.

My favorite artist is Edward Kienholz, a sculptor who passed away in 1994. I call him the Warren Zevon of art because his works told a story. He was as much a journalist as he was an artist. His greatest work in my eyes was The Beanery, a life-size, walk-in art installation he created in 1965. It basically re-created the inside and part of the outside of Barney's Beanery, located in West Hollywood, and which is still around today.

As you enter The Beanery, there is a newsstand by the front door with a Los Angeles Herald Examiner newspaper from 1965 about US involvement in the

Vietnam War. The headline says "Children Kill Children in Vietnam Riots."

Once inside you hear noise but you can't understand a word being said. It's recordings of idle bar chatter.

It could be any bar in America. There are wax figures of bartenders behind the bar pouring drinks and there are wax figures of people sitting at the bar ordering drinks. One catch. Almost everybody has a clock for a face and everybody's face tells the same time, 10:10 p.m. There is even a male and female paired off at the bar—as in any bar in America—with the male lighting a cigarette for the female.

The most controversial part of the installation is the sign on the bar which says "Faggots-Stay Out!" This sign is ironic, considering Barney's Beanery sits in the middle of gay West Hollywood. You have to remember this was 1965. The sign in the real Barney's Beanery is long gone today.

I would have loved to have a twosome in the middle of The Beanery but I could never get in there or try to hide in there without other people standing in line outside the installation ready to enter. But it always stuck in my mind, so with my newfound cache of lottery money, I had a sculptor make a "Beanery Bartender" out of wax and put a clock on her, telling the same 10:10 p.m. time. But one difference, I had it booby-trapped. I knew exactly how I was going to use it when the time came.

Now, let me tell you about the ugly, violent, unattractive, obnoxious side of art that I despise.

Tattoos. What a waste. What's the point? Yes, you want a nice little object on a part of your body carefully hidden from view but meaningful to you, fine. I'll even go as far as to say, to some people, that would be considered art.

But a sleeve of tats? Are you serious? There is nothing artistic about that. It's clutter, not art. Somebody should cut off your arm and place it in one of those storage bags you can deflate and store away for posterity. You have all those tattoos, you're an idiot. Why do I say that? Well, dumbshit, you just took yourself out of the mainstream.

Any chance you had of working for a major corporation; any chance you had of appearing in a TV commercial; any chance you had of even being a server in a high-class restaurant, you blew it. You cut off your income possibilities big time. You're just stupid. You want to seem cool; you want to seem hip for today's crowd.

Congratulations, Mr. Hipster, Miss Cool, you are now perfect material for a fast food or maybe a mixed martial arts career.

I met one of these tattoo dudes, ironically, at a museum. Rory or Roger or something like that. Bald head. The following on his back: A large tiger that covered pretty much his entire back. Next to it down the right side was a large giraffe. On the other side of the tiger was a unicorn. Around all three of these so-called poetic tattoos, were those braided barbed wire configurations.

Running down his right arm he had the names of three different women. I sure hope they were relatives instead of past girlfriends. On his left arm, he had a skeleton's head sitting on a bible, with a couple of biblical verses written above it that you couldn't read unless you looked real close, and then some other figures which I also had a hard time figuring out.

A tattoo guy with a dumb sense of self-worth in a modern art museum? I was curious. I introduced myself and we talked about the various contemporary art pieces on hand. Lichtenstein, Warhol, Vasserely, and some people I never heard of.

"Do you consider those tattoos on your back and arm art?"

"Oh absolutely. A contemporary piece of art. As good as some of the pieces in here."

"But you can't tell what some of the art is. Forgive me, but it looks more like clutter to me than art."

"I agree. But I know what it is and that is the most important thing. And anybody who gets close to me will know what these figures are."

"Why do you come to these museums?"

"I get ideas about other figures I can put on my body. My goal is to cover about seventy-five percent of my entire body."

"Mainstream corporate America, I'm sure is waiting for that."

"I lost mainstream corporate America a long time ago. But it's not important. I train some mixed martial arts fighters and I feel I need to identify with them."

"I could never figure that out. Which comes first the tattoo or the mixed martial artist? In other words, did your guys already have the tattoos and then decide to train for

MMA, or were they MMA fighters and to fit in, they decided to add some tattoos to their body."

"I vote for the latter. MMA guys first and tattoos second. Although you are right, some people have overdone the tattoo collection, including yours truly."

I invited him back to my new house. No more condo for me. The money I won in the lottery allowed me to make a nice down payment on an upscale house in Spanish Hills, just west of Spanish Trails, off Tropicana.

We rolled around in my new Casper king-size bed. Much more room than my old queen. He got on top of me. He wanted to go inside me and in his words "ground and pound." I wasn't in the mood for sexual intercourse with him, so I asked him to give me his opinion of the Beanery Bartender I had commissioned. He went over, the clock lit up, he touched the clock and that was all she wrote. The clock set off one of those vacuum plastic bags that immediately covered his face. The bag started to deflate, trapping his head inside. He was about to suffocate. I enjoyed watching him try and fight it.

Eventually, he had to tap out for good. I dragged him to my car in the garage, and took him to Rock A Hoola Water Park, gave him one of my proper burials, stopped at The Lottery Store on the way back, bought a large bottle of Diet Pepsi without aspartame, and two lottery tickets, neither of which garnered me any money. Oh, well, just another good date night and another notch on my bedside scoreboard.

Chapter Thirteen

Are They Closing In?

A m I remorseful when I eliminate one of my new friends? Not really. I mean, I have a scoreboard behind my bed that I mark to congratulate myself on the number of kills I have totaled up so the time for remorse should come right before the kill, not after. If I don't want that person to die, I don't kill them. I don't finish the job. I let them live and we all go on with our lives.

As I was about to take Tattoo Man to Rock-A-Hoola, I turned on the TV and was met with some bad news. The FBI had dug up more of Rock-A-Hoola and found three more bodies. So, counting Bozo the Clown, that made four.

My mistake for burying them so close together. There were probably about ten or twelve bodies I had buried there now but luckily I divided them into different areas.

This was the first time I was worried about the FBI finding some stray DNA. My DNA. The local newspapers and TV stations were talking about a serial killer. Because of the DNA, they learned the identities of the four people they had found. All were from out of town and all had been reported missing. Luckily for me, they had not found any of my DNA. If they expanded their search and found the other seven or eight, I may be in trouble. I needed to be more careful. I needed to find another burial location. Rock-A-Hoola had served its purpose but it was time to move on.

My next choice of a burial ground was the Las Vegas Archers camp. This was a private large target area between Las Vegas and Pahrump. For those of you that don't know, Pahrump is where most of the legal brothels are located. It's about forty-five minutes from the Las Vegas Strip.

This was a lot shorter of a drive than Rock-A-Hoola. I took the 15 freeway to Blue Diamond Road. Then I headed west about twenty miles, passing a brown motorhome that looked unattended, a fire station and a sign warning me, "Watch out for Wild Horses and Boars." The range was locked with a key lock but I became a master of sorts about two years ago with easy locks such as this one. I don't think I could ever open a bank safe but these type of locks that you would normally find on backyard gates or garages were fairly easy to conquer.

The Las Vegas Archery Range had two types of targets. The normal colorful targets with the bull's eyes taped to bales of hay, and the 3D range which consisted of high-density foam animals such as deer, boars, bobcats, foxes, beavers and lions, among others.

To get to the 3D range you pass a cabin or two, which I assume was where the archers held their meetings; an outhouse and signs telling you that this was the dirt intersection of Van Marshall Blvd and Mary Lynn Way.

I do not know who Van and Mary were but I'm sure they must have meant a great deal to the Las Vegas Archers in order to get those street signs made up.

The dirt here was much softer than Rock-A-Hoola. Burials would be much quicker. I took the 3D route and spotted my first animal, a beige deer complete with horns. It was about five feet tall and about six or seven feet wide, and was up a hill maybe twenty-five yards from me.

I drove up that hill maybe ten yards, made a quick left turn off the trail about twenty feet, found a soft section of dirt and decided this is where I would bury my next victim. This location served me well. It was closer to town, more isolated, had a much larger footprint and was easier to dig up than Rock-A-Hoola. I think even the archers who would hike up and down this land on weekends would have a tough time coming across my dead bodies accidentally.

The only negative was that I missed my trips to The Lottery Store. I'd have to find somewhere else to stop if I needed a diet Pepsi without aspartame.

☙Chapter Fourteen❧

I Look Pretty and Can Kick You in the Head

Because of my lottery winnings, I decided I didn't need to take as many modeling gigs at trade shows and conventions, although I still tried to do one show a week. Every Wednesday I would take a kickboxing class, and I was getting good at it. I have long legs, so I can reach high with them, enough to kick someone in the face or head and probably knock them out.

Before you get to the point of being able to kick someone in the head you had to pass a few tests. First, you had to face off with "Bob." Bob is a mannequin with an adjustable height from five feet tall to about seven feet tall. It has vinyl skin, looks like a bully and doesn't fight back.

He was no match for my barefoot kicks to his head. But he kept bouncing back, never going down until one of my roundhouse kicks flattened him. The next step was to kick a paddle the instructor would bring out and hold high.

My legs are strong and flexible and it feels great to me to be able to kick that high and reach not only one paddle the instructor was holding high over my head but a second one he was holding with his other hand.

61

I developed a friendship with several of the guys and girls in the class. Usually, there were the same people every week, so you would acknowledge people you knew and sometimes you would all get a smoothie after class. My favorite was the Kiwi Quencher.

I booked a beauty convention at the Las Vegas Convention Center for the weekend. This convention had makeup products, skincare products, eye creams, eyeliners, hair products, finger and toenail polish, etc.

Even though most people walking around at these conventions represent retail stores, a lot of women attend to get the scoop on what crap is coming out next to help make them look twenty years younger.

None of this bothered me. It was my job to pass out brochures from the nail polish company I was modeling for. Either that or set up a meeting with a retail buyer and a sales executive.

What did bother me were all these so-called influencers running around the beauty convention thinking they were important. I passed a sign that said, "Connecting brands and influencers to help women be their best version." What a pile of crap.

There were influencer meet and greets, influencer dinners, even Influencer Choice Awards all geared to publicize certain products with certain people. The older women, forty to sixty, would pay big bucks to meet and hang out with these young influencers.

I'm not sure why. It's not like they would automatically look younger. Maybe they were hoping for free samples.

It amazes me that companies think that influencers influence. I wouldn't buy a thing because a so-called influencer endorsed it. It's the same with athletes. Just because an athlete uses a certain product, doesn't mean that product is good. To me, it means the company thinks there are lots of gullible people out there so they will pay an athlete or some model a large fee to promote their products. Again, the stupidity of the American buyer sometimes stuns me.

At this convention, influencers were mainly these attractive model types who have a million Instagram followers and expect their followers to do, say and buy anything they promote. Of course, I remember reading about this teenage girl who had over a million followers and in order to get a company to pay her a large influencer fee they asked her to try and sell just thirty-five to forty purses. She couldn't sell that many. Oh too bad.

Fame is so fleeting.

And the best story I read about came from the Los Angeles Times. It told of a young man who opened a food truck to sell soft ice cream. Nothing special just a family recipe of chocolate, vanilla and a swirl of the two. But these influencers came by with offers such as "I don't know if you know me but I have 100,000 followers. Could you hook me up with ice cream? I'll post about you in my next story."

The ice-cream vendor was at first "confused" considering it was only a four-dollar product. Eventually, he got pissed at all the free requests, so he made a sign and stuck it on his truck. "Influencers Pay Double." I applaud this entrepreneur. I think a lot of us are confused that influencers think they have real influence. They are just freeloaders in my eyes.

Across the aisle from me was Angel Heaven—oh, we all know, it was surely her real name—and she was the official influencer for Angel lipstick which "comes in twenty-nine flavors." Angel was there to sign autographs, give out samples of #19 Heavenly Peach and I assume add to her Instagram followers list.

We both had our lunch break at the same time, so I struck up a conversation with her. I asked her how she got so many followers.

"You just put your best photos out there, and people want to connect with you. A lot of them are men who think they can F you. But a lot of them are women or younger teenagers who aspire to be as pretty as you. You end up developing a following. Of course, it helps that I did a YouTube show once a week giving tips on how to apply lipstick and what lipstick colors go with what outfits. Then this lipstick company came to me, offered me a $100,000 annual contract, and named a brand after me. Angel Lipstick."

We hit it off, had dinner together and she invited me up to her hotel room, a nice suite at The Palms. I'm attracted to men but I could see she liked women, so I decided to just ride it out. Sure enough, she bought two small bottles of Ketel One vodka from the mini bar, added some cranberry juice and I assume added some kind of Bill Cosby pill to sedate me. I drank one sip of the mixed drink but when she wasn't paying attention I dumped the rest out in a nearby plant.

I pretended to be groggy and laid back down on the bed. She waited until I looked asleep and she got on me, started kissing me and fondling my breasts. I didn't have any problem with that but when she dove for my pubic area and started to play with it, I stopped this charade.

I pushed her off me, told her I was not one of the people she could influence and started to put on my clothes to leave.

She got up, called me a bitch, and threw a right hook that glanced off the side of my face. Enough is enough. I threw a roundhouse kick to her head and knocked her out. I sure hope she made it to the convention the next day. Heaven forbid if her followers weren't around to see their favorite influencer with a black and blue mark on her face. On my way out, I took one of her lipstick samples, #22, Perfect Pink. I figured she owed me that.

ᴄᴊᴏChapter Fifteenᴄᴏ

When I Kill You, I'm Pretty Sure You're Dead

There he was laying peacefully on my bed. Dead. Or so I thought. His name was Roger or Robert or something like that. Mid-thirties, some kind of sales position, in Las Vegas for a convention. I was working the convention as a promotional model, met him, he took me to dinner, and one thing led to another.

I ran out of some of the ingredients I use for my toxic concoctions, so I had to improvise. When I applied the ointment to his chest and rubbed it in, it seemed to run quickly through his bloodstream, and he was out within a minute or two. I thought no problem. Rest in peace, my friend. I'll get ready for a drive up to the archery camp and give him the proper burial. Then maybe fifteen minutes later he started snoring. It startled me. I thought the guy was dead but he was making a comeback.

I've never been in a situation where someone comes back from the dead. When I kill them, they stay killed. Sounds corny, I know. But there is always a first time. I decided to end it by taking a Malouf gel-infused memory foam pillow with a Zimasilk 100% Silk Mulberry pillowcase, twenty-nine dollars at most stores, cheaper at Amazon, and put it over his face.

Then I leaned back against my headboard, stretched out and put both my feet on the pillow and pressed hard. It took another half-minute before he ran out of air and this time I felt his pulse to make sure he was dead.

I took the drive to the archery range, found a side road by the colorful bullseye targets, and buried him in a corner behind a tree.

On my way back to Las Vegas, I saw a sign for a new exhibition called The Gallery of Death and Life and based on what just happened that evening, it piqued my curiosity enough that I decided to go see it the next day.

This was one of those traveling exhibitions that Mandalay Bay Hotel brought in. Ever since the massacre that took place when a deranged gunman broke out a window on the thirty-second floor in October 2017, and started arbitrarily shooting people at the Route 91 Harvest Music Festival across the street, occupancy at Mandalay Bay has suffered.

To make up for it, the hotel brings in more events, concerts and exhibitions. Even the famed Foundation Room, which at one time was the best private club in town, became just another public venue where they could charge money for anybody to get in. I had a friend who was a member from the beginning, over nineteen years, until he found out he couldn't even get a seat to watch the Super Bowl at his own club without buying a table.

He decided not to renew his membership. I don't blame him. So, I bought a ticket to The Gallery of Death and Life, and I have to admit it, I was fascinated.

The first tableau was a replica of the Golden Gate Bridge with a guy falling off it. True story. The first person to fall off the Golden Gate Bridge actually survived.

His name was Slim and he was a construction worker, who accidentally slipped and fell off the bridge into the water. He survived the fall with injuries, but his life intact. After that he became the luckiest guy alive. He was paid to be on the cover of a Wheaties Cereal box. He was paid to endorse Camel cigarettes and he wound up on most every news show in the country. He became famous and with that he became rich. He moved to Hawaii and wound up as one of the top yacht racers in the country.

The next tableau was another interesting death-to-life person, Maggie Dickinson.

Maggie was sentenced to be hung in 1724 in Edinburgh, Scotland for having a child out of wedlock and "killing it." Actually, the child was stillborn, so it wasn't her fault. They hung her and according to history, her body remained suspended for 30 minutes before they took her away in a coffin. She started making noises while in the coffin, and when they opened it up, she was still breathing. She eventually was granted a full pardon, and evidently, to this day there is still a pub named after her in the city of Edinburgh.

I moved from room to room. You had the woman in South Africa who was involved in a car crash and declared dead only to wake up in a morgue refrigerator; and this one I liked the best, a prisoner in Spain was found unconscious in his cell and declared dead by three forensic doctors. Four hours later, on the autopsy table, and with the markings already on his body ready for cutting, he began to snore. Oops.

According to doctors, at least the competent ones, a person is legally dead when his or her heart stops beating or they are considered brain dead, meaning no electrical impulses are being sent to brain cells. But if you are not a doctor, I'm sure it's tough to make that call.

This exhibition caused me to think about my kill sheet. Except for the previous night, did anybody I kill ever wake up after I thought I had eliminated them. Nope, I was certain. But what about after I had buried them? I'm pretty sure that never happened. I suppose if the guy woke up and survived, he would be walking around Rock-A-Hoola like a zombie until somebody discovered him. Then the local papers and news stations would hear about it from the local police. This has not happened yet, and like I said, I'm not going to worry about it.

☙Chapter Sixteen❧

Boxing Day on Mulholland Drive

I'm a pretty decent athlete. Did some swimming, wrestling and track and field in high school. Nothing spectacular. No championships. When I got to college, I gave up sports, and because I looked decent, I was asked to join the cheerleading squad.

But, as I said earlier, I've become fairly proficient at kickboxing. I take a class once every week, sometimes twice. I use it for exercise and self-defense. But I never thought I would use it for a competition.

A friend of mine in Los Angeles knew of a magazine publisher who would throw all women's boxing or kickboxing matches in the backyard of his house in a gated community off Mulholland Drive in Beverly Hills. Take my word for it, it was a big backyard. He set up five matches on a Sunday morning, three of them boxing, two of them kickboxing. He would pair the women by weight and experience. Each winner would get $1000, each loser $500.

I was asked by my friend if I wanted to participate. My opponent would be in her 20s and had a 3-1 boxing record but this would be her first kickboxing match. I said I'd give it a try.

This entire event was legal. The publisher had to get a promoter's license and he had to get all matches approved by the California State Athletic Commission. The three-ring judges and referee had to be licensed and approved as well.

This was a great event if I do say so myself. Maybe 100 people in attendance. A lot of celebrities. A standard size boxing ring was set up. The mat was a little bouncy, better to protect someone's head if a knockout came. And there would be an intermission after the third bout so everybody could head to the bagel brunch buffet the publisher had set up.

I was in the third bout. My opponent was a better boxer than me but she probably wasn't going to throw many kicks. I figured I better stay at a distance and hope I could connect my foot to her head. And that's exactly what I did. In the first round, she jabbed me and jabbed me and jabbed me with her left, keeping me off balance. I knew a right hook was coming, so I stayed away from her. But she connected and I went down.

I wasn't hurt, so I got up and was given a standing eight count. Again she kept me off balance with left-handed jabs. I didn't want to go down again, so I figured I better do something. I took a step back and swung a spinning roundhouse kick that connected to her head. Boom she went down for the full ten count.

Hooray for me. I won, collected my $1,000 prize and decided my kickboxing career had come to a close. Undefeated.

At the bagel brunch, there was a lot of what I would call boxing groupies. Guys who wanted to date women who were attractive yet tough. Guys who loved the idea that their new girlfriend could control the relationship in the bedroom. These men were successful so the girlfriend wouldn't be controlling their careers. But after stressful days, a lot of these men wanted the woman to take charge in the bedroom behind closed doors.

I met Freddy. An agent for a medium-sized talent agency. He handled a lot of B actors and actresses. This guy was weak in relation to women I could tell. He kept hinting for me to throw a roundhouse kick at his head. Not there. But back at his Encino home. He wanted to go out with me. Dinner and a kickboxing lesson. He would pay me $500. I didn't need the money but I said ok.

The next night he picked me up at my hotel, took me to Dan Tana's on Santa Monica Blvd. for an Italian dinner, and then we went back to his house. He lived by himself. He had a basketball hoop in his backyard, a swing set with a slide above a pool, and a boxing ring, of course.

He kissed me, I kissed back. He put me on the swing and swung me high. I hated it and after a few seconds, I asked him to stop. When I was a kid, my parents had a swing set in our backyard, and one day, I was maybe eight or nine, I went on it, swung myself high and fast, and accidentally fell forward and hit the ground. I had the wind knocked out of me. I was scared. That was the first time I was fighting for breath. I had to gasp and gasp and gasp to get my breath back. But from then on, I couldn't go on a swing set again. If I swung, I would feel the sensation of my breath leaving me, even if I didn't swing fast or high.

He asked me to go into the ring with him. We put on boxing gloves. He started jabbing at me with no power behind it. I followed with a couple of kicks to his stomach, and head. Then followed those with a light front kick to his groin. No harm intended. I could tell he got hard as soon as that happened. This was what he wanted all along. To be overpowered in a sexual way. I said sorry and told him I could make it feel better. I went over to him, rubbed my hand down his crotch and kissed him. He wanted me to join him in his master bedroom, which I did.

I excused myself, went to the bathroom, and brought out a little jar from my purse, which sometimes I fondly refer to as Love Potion #8. I told him to lay down, and then still with my boxing gloves on, I proceeded to rub his penis lightly with my potion.

He got hard again. He almost released right there. But it wouldn't be long now.

The poison was going into his bloodstream.

"Do you believe in God?" I asked him.

"I'm not so sure. Maybe there is one, maybe not. I don't really care."

"Interesting. You're the first person I've gone out with that is not so sure God exists."

Under normal circumstances, I may have let him live. But it was too late. He began clutching his throat. He asked for some water. I went to the kitchen and gave him some water. But the poison had already kicked in. He passed away very peacefully. I kissed him on the lips and I actually whispered "I'm sorry."

Oh well, can't worry about it now. Even though this was in the San Fernando Valley, it was still a four and one-half hour drive back to Las Vegas. When I got back within city limits, I made the drive to the archery range with my new friend in the trunk, found a nice spot to bury him, and I actually cried a little bit because he was a nice guy.

On the drive back to my house, I was thinking about who I'd like for my next victim. Nobody would be better suited than O.J. Simpson.

ᏟᏐChapter SeventeenᏟᏐ

Facebook Friend My Ass

After a long drive from Encino back to Las Vegas, and an archery range burial, I went straight to sleep. I slept ten hours. I needed it. Killing somebody takes a lot out of you. Mentally and physically. After waking up, I turned on my computer and went on Facebook. I don't look at Facebook every day. Maybe about once or twice a week. The only time I post on it is when I've gone to a new club or new restaurant or watch a new movie.

Obviously, I keep my private life private.

But when I turned on Facebook this time, I was greeted with an unusual friend request. Now, I've had a lot of friend requests—and most of them I accept even if I don't know the person. But this one stood out.

It was from O. J. Simpson. No shit.

Of all people who would want to connect with me, I never expected an alleged murderer to do so. Ironic, isn't it? I've killed more people than this asshole but I would never consider being his friend.

Wouldn't it be great if I was the one who did kill him? I thought.

75

I'd find an ironic place to bury him, maybe on the grounds of the new Las Vegas Raiders Stadium. I would be famous, for sure, but that's exactly what I didn't want. I don't need the fame. I don't need the glory.

I met him at a Christmas party given by one of my model friends.

He was dressed in a sport coat and tie. He, of course, introduced himself to all the models at the party. He was polite. We struck up a conversation about promotional modeling work and he eventually asked me out to dinner. I politely declined.

I told him that a friend of mine who used to play pro football for the Pittsburgh Steelers told me he had been over to his house in Brentwood once on 4th of July for a party and all the girls in attendance would be thrown in the pool. Even if you didn't have on a bathing suit, you'd get thrown in. Clothes and all.

"That wasn't nice," I told him.

"All in good fun," he said. "Nobody got hurt."

I've always wondered what Mr. Simpson thinks about when he's at a social gathering. In the back of his mind, is he thinking "these people really don't like me because they know I'm a killer." Is it affecting his relationships, business, social or otherwise? Is it affecting how he talks to people? Is he trying to overcompensate by being a polite gentleman? What would happen if one of the models went up to him and said, "Hi Killer. Anybody strike your fancy tonight? Do you need to borrow a knife?"

Now, talk about a guy I'd love to kill. By the time I got through with him, we wouldn't need another trial. But it wasn't safe for me to do that. He was known by too many people and word would have gotten out who he had gone out with. Even if we went back to a hotel instead of my house or his house, it was too dangerous.

Out of curiosity, I looked at his friends on Facebook. He had over 2,000. Nobody famous I could see. All the men looked as if they were out of Hillbilly Row. Messy, no professional jobs to speak of. I would probably murder any of these guys if I could, but the problem was I never ran into any of them. I don't think they had the brains to find a way to meet me in normal social circles. As for the women, I only saw a handful, and they were porn stars, hookers or strippers. Yep, that's the type of girl attracted to Mr. Simpson these days.

I went to the store and bought a dozen large rainbow lollipops. These suckers were big. I had something in mind to use them in the future.

I turned on the TV and was again met with some bad news. The FBI had dug up more of Rock-A-Hoola and found three more bodies.

My mistake for burying them closer together than I thought. There were I'm sure a dozen bodies give or take there now total. Once again, I was worried about the FBI finding some stray DNA. My DNA. The local newspapers and TV stations were talking about a serial killer. Because of the DNA, they learned the identities of most of the people they had found. All were from out of town and all had been reported missing. Once again, because I wear gloves, luckily for me, they had not found any of my DNA.

Chapter Eighteen

We Haven't Grown Up Yet

I was getting paid $500 a day for five days to attend Comic Con in San Diego and dress up like Black Widow, the Scarlett Johansson character in all the Avenger films.

Scarlett was in attendance herself but only to make a brief appearance and talk to the press. I was her stand-in so to speak at Marvel's booth on the convention floor.

I had to dye my hair dark red, and they sent me a kind of cool all-leather black outfit, including black leather belt and black leather knee-high boots. I would stand there and let people take photos with me. I would say seventy percent of the photos were with men.

Comic Con is one of the most successful conventions in the country, drawing 135,000 people annually, about twenty-five per cent of them dressed in some kind of costume.

For those who want to make a comparison, the famous Consumer Electronics Show, which makes an annual appearance in Las Vegas, draws around 125,000 with about ninety percent of them dressed as nerds. In the old days, Comic Con was geared for comic book collectors.

Mom and Pop stores would bring out all their old comics, pile them in old boxes and sell to anyone who collected. This was not a sophisticated convention early on.

Later on, the TV networks and film studios got smart and started to promote their shows at Comic Con. They would bring their A-list celebrities to the convention, set up a panel discussion in Hall H and show a trailer for whatever was coming next. Don't underestimate these panel discussions. Hall H holds 7,000 people and panels in this hall would come close to full capacity. No mistaking this, it was big business. No mom and pop boxes here.

Marvel, the people paying me, decided to forego the usual panels this time.

Instead, they introduced their upcoming slate of films and brought on the celebs attached to them. "Natalie Portman come on down. Please welcome Angelina Jolie. Say hello to Scarlett Johansson. Mahershala Ali please join us."

Back on the convention floor, there were still some smaller stores selling old comic books but most of the booths had given up on comic books in favor of toys. Plush animals, dolls, anything that looked like one of the superheroes was up for sale.

So who buys this crap? Adults, that's who. Oh, maybe some are bought by parents for their kids. But most are bought by adults who treat them as collectibles and hope that one day they will increase in value.

Of course, I met a lot of people here dressed in all kinds of outfits or costumes. I was attracted to one guy. And I could tell he liked me because he kept coming around every hour or so to take a photo. He was dressed in a suit that was designed to look like red bricks.

I had a forty-five minute break so he offered to buy me a hamburger. They don't offer a gourmet menu at these conventions. We went off to an empty room on the second floor of the San Diego Convention Center. They must have had a panel in it earlier because there were some old comic books left on the table where the panelists would sit. Elektra, Black Widow, Catwoman, Wonder Woman and one I had never heard of titled Chantilly Lace who was unbeatable and dangerous with a bow and arrow. This must have been a panel for female superheroes.

"I wish I could have sat in on this panel," I said to my new friend as yet unnamed.

"Me too. I was so busy running around at the booths, I forgot this was going on," he said.

"You mean you were so busy admiring me in my Black Widow costume that it slipped your mind."

"Guilty."

"Why do so many adults collect these comic books, or these figurines," I asked.

"I mean they are just toys. Kids' stuff. Yeah, I know they are collectibles. I don't think people really collect these to see if their value goes up. I think they sleep with them under their pillows."

"A lot of us haven't grown up yet, some people obviously more than others. A lot of people live vicariously through comic books, but when you see and have a chance to be with a real person, and that person is as beautiful as you, these comic books have to take a back seat."

"Thank you for the compliment," I said. "What do you do in real life?"

"I'm almost famous," he said. "My name is Paul Kilkenny. Have you ever heard of me?"

"Yeah, sure, you were one of 73 candidates running for president."

"No, I'm serious," he said. "They used to call me 'Cup of Coffee' Kilkenny."

"Sorry Paul, doesn't ring a bell."

"I was a professional baseball player. Played eight years in the minors. Could never make the majors. Then one weekend, the final weekend of the season, my parent club The San Diego Padres called me up, figuring I may be retiring at the end of the season and I should at least get a chance to experience the 'Bigs.' So on the second to last game of the season, they started me in right field. I ended up hitting three home runs that night and made a diving catch in the outfield. The fans gave me a standing ovation, I got to keep my uniform and my career was done."

"Didn't they play you the next day?"

"Nope. They said I could never duplicate that so I should just go out a hero."

"So why the nickname Cup of Coffee Kilkenny?"

"When a baseball player has a short major league career, and believe me, you couldn't get much shorter than mine, they say he was up in the majors for a 'Cup of Coffee.' I take it endearingly. At least I made it. So many people don't."

"Seems to me you could have parlayed that into an endorsement contract with some coffee company," I said.

"Oh I did and I still do. Starbucks gives me an annual fee for whatever they need me for. Store openings, TV commercials, appearances at the annual convention of owners. And all the coffee I can drink. Their first contract was $175,000 per year plus expenses. Now, I'm at a flat $75,000 annually. I'm really not complaining. It's decent for a guy who played in one major league baseball game in his entire life."

"So tell me, do you really drink Starbucks coffee?"

"My drink of choice when I go into one of their stores is an Iced Grande Chai Tea Latte. But there are times when it's cold I order a Caffe Latte. I really do like their coffee."

"And when you are not plugging coffee, what do you do?"

"I sell insurance. Nothing glamorous but it pays the bills until I can find a real career I enjoy."

"What would you enjoy?"

"I'd love to do color commentary for a baseball team. Minors, majors, it doesn't matter. I've been taking some radio classes and practicing a lot. The Padres let me sit in an isolated press box during any day game and practice calling the game into a microphone and tape deck."

My lunchtime was drawing to a close. Cup of Coffee Kilkenny would live to see another day. I thanked him for the hamburger and we made tentative plans to see each other next time he made it to Las Vegas.

ᴄ⁓Chapter Nineteen⁓ᴐ

The Barber Shoppe

My girlfriend Kerrie called me up and asked me if I wanted to meet her at this new place in the Cosmopolitan Hotel called The Barber Shoppe. She told me I would like the place because it was full of surprises. I told her I would see her at 9:00 p.m. Just past the Chandelier Bar with the iconic somewhat gaudy chandelier made of over two million crystal beads, I spotted The Barber Shoppe. But just before the entrance into The Barber Shoppe I came across a really cool sculpture of a woman in what is called The Pose. The Pose is where a woman is laying on her stomach with her head down or slightly raised and her feet raised up crossed. This is the favorite position of guys with a foot fetish because you see the girls' soles.

The head and torso of the sculpture were made with thick wires of different colors each carefully wrapped around the woman's head and body. The ankles and feet—the lower half of The Pose—were made with those same colorful wires but around her legs were martial arts belts of all colors. White, yellow, red, green, blue, brown and black.

I took a couple of photos in case I wanted a similar, smaller sculpture made for my house and walked into The Barber Shoppe.

You walk in and there are three old-fashioned barber chairs with real barbers and men sitting in the chairs I assume getting a real haircut or straight razor shave. On the walls were old-time photos of old-time barbers and old-time barber poles. Each barber's chair offered a direct view of a TV with as you could imagine a sports event on. The sign on the wall that I thought was clever read, "Shave Without Pain or Whiskers Refunded."

Just past the barber's chairs was a door marked "Janitor." You open this door and the world changes. You have entered a cool-looking lounge.

On one side is the bar with the usual bar stools. In the middle are couches geared for couples and larger parties. At the back is a stage with band instruments on it. They have live music on Fridays and Saturdays and Karaoke on Thursdays.

On the other side of the room are three barber's chairs. Behind each barber's chair is an Asian model holding either a knife or scissors and each wearing a shirt that says, "I'll Cut You." I'm assuming the Asian models knew how to cut hair.

Just past the Asian models is another door. There is nothing written on this door. But I opened it and walked into a small restaurant that probably seats no more than twenty people. Inside I see a couple in their thirties eating steak and lobster. I wasn't hungry, so I went back into the bar where I found Kerrie.

Kerrie and I drank the night away. Not too much for me. I am not someone who gets drunk. At the bar was one of those old Barbicide containers that would normally hold some cleaning solvent to clean the barber's combs and brushes. In this case they held cooked bacon. Yep, you just open up the container and you get a nice fresh piece of bacon just in case you get hungry. The bar also had some fresh oranges and strawberries on the counter you could nibble on.

Guys were coming up to us, chitchatting, and buying us drinks, so we accepted. It was now 2:00 a.m. The Barber Shoppe closes at 2:00 a.m. unlike most other bars in Las Vegas that stay open until the last person leaves.

Kerrie and I hugged each other, and she left. I sat there and finished my drink. I didn't see anybody else in the bar except the servers, bartenders and one fat security guy. I went to the restroom and about sixty seconds later the fat security guy came in and asked me to take off my clothes. "No thank you. I'm going to leave now. I love this place. I promise I'll be back."

"I'm going to give you a going away party you'll never forget."

He started to come toward me and I kneed him in the groin. He grabbed me, started to kiss me, and then just ripped off part of my top.

"As long as you have some of your clothes off, you might as well take off the rest," he said.

I didn't give him a chance to get any closer. I had just enough room to do a spinning back kick—thank goodness for my kickboxing classes—and connected with his head. The kick knocked him out. I went back in the bar. No one was there now.

I grabbed a large plastic bag filled with oranges, placed the oranges in a dish, and went back into the bathroom and placed the bag over the head of the fat security guard and pulled until I could see there was no breath coming out of this mouth or nose. "You damned scumbag, you got what you deserved."

I wasn't going to take any chances that I would be seen on a security camera, so I called security and told them what had happened.

"This asshole was going to do bad things to me," I told the hotel security guy. I explained everything in detail. They could see how my clothes were ripped.

They took my statement. And let me go.

"Just let me know if you need anything further from me," I said.

As I've said before, when you know how to do something well, it just gets easier.

Kerrie called me the next day.

"Did you hear the news about the security guard who was killed at The Barber Shoppe? That was after I left."

"Sorry, you missed all the excitement. But you're speaking to the one who did the killing."

"What? What happened?"

"The asshole tried to rape me in the bathroom. I knocked him out with a roundhouse kick and then put a plastic bag over his head and he suffocated," I said.

"Why didn't they arrest you?"

"I talked to hotel security and then to the cops. I told them what happened and showed them how he ripped my dress."

"But you killed the guy."

"I told them I didn't mean to kill anyone. I was scared. I just wanted to make sure he was out and he wouldn't get up and continue to try and rape me. The cops took down my information and let me go."

In my own mind, I was getting good at this.

Chapter Twenty

Las Vegas the City of Death

If there was any place that reminded me of death it was Las Vegas. I thought this was a perfect city for me to partake in my hobby. Las Vegas doesn't give a shit about people. It's only concerned about money.

I remember one guy having a heart attack by the slot machines in a casino and nobody coming to his aid. They were too concerned about their slot bets, craps bets, their poker hands, and where the spinning ball on the roulette wheel would land.

In the old days, if someone would commit suicide by jumping off a hotel roof, by agreement, the newspapers and TV stations would not report it. Heaven forbid if this city got a bad name. We don't want anything to take away from the tourist trade, our main source of income. Today, it seems, journalism has prevailed, and if someone dies in a hotel or casino, it is covered by the media.

The conventions and trade shows are geared for out-of-towners. Usually, midwestern store owners who would rarely get to see celebrities in their own home town, so they look forward to getting out to Vegas once a year.

I felt that some of these people were staring at death's door and were looking forward to seeing this city before they passed away. I remember a woman I met on my trip to Cleveland who said, "Before I die, I'm going to get to see Las Vegas." I thought *"why don't you just get on a plane with one of your girlfriends or cousins and just go, it's not that big of a deal."* But evidently, it is a big deal to some, something special.

This week I am at a wedding convention. You'll love this. Every day at 2:00 p.m. I get married. Same groom, same preacher, same ceremony. We kiss after every wedding, and the people who watch would invariably cry. After our ceremony, I hand out small packets of tissues. And as a nice added touch, I throw the bouquet of flowers to some unsuspecting woman. The person who catches the bouquet gets $50 off anything that is being sold at my booth.

On the final day of the convention, I met Mr. Weddingman. That's what his business card said. He was a guy from Springfield, Missouri who would charge $10,000 for a video of each wedding and reception he was hired to attend. He promised to make the video look like it was Entertainment Tonight covering it. He had an on-camera hostess interview the bride and groom and many of the guests. He would treat the guests as celebrities.

"Over here we have Milt Mahaffey, the personal plumber for the Robindale couple," the hostess would say.

"Tell us Milt. Do the Robindales have a fancy bathroom? I've heard they have a sunken beige tub for two." And so on. Milt would answer and the on-camera hostess would move on to the next "celebrity."

Mr. Weddingman told me I would be a great on-camera hostess and he would like to audition me to see if I could do it. Of course, that audition would need to take place back at his hotel room.

"Let's go to my place instead. I have a nice house, bigger than your hotel room."

"OK, I'll see you at 7:00. Once we finish the audition I'll take you out for a nice sushi dinner," he said. He brought a small video camera and one light. He gave me a script to read while he was setting up. He turned on the camera and I did my read. I think I was pretty decent. But I knew this guy was not going to hire me. He just wanted to have sex.

"You did a great job," he said.

"What a liar," I thought to myself.

"I think I can use you one of these days," he added.

"Do I have enough experience?" I asked. "I've modeled a lot but no one has asked me to be a spokesperson."

"Not hard to do. We'll just have to practice a few times before you do it for real."

"I'm interested. When can we practice?"

"Well, I'm out here for a wedding about every two or three weeks," he said. "It would be nice if we could get together every time I come out."

He walked up to me and kissed me. I wasn't interested in the guy. So I just gave him one of those quick Hollywood kisses and told him we should take it slow.

I thanked him, told him I was looking forward to working with him, and said we should celebrate by having one of my large lollipops before we went out for some sushi. I unwrapped the lollipop for him, gave him another Hollywood kiss on the lips, rolled the lollipop around his lips and stuck it in his mouth.

He licked and licked and licked, took a small bite, then he choked up, spit some of the sucker out of his mouth, fell to the floor, went into a couple of convulsions and died.

I took him to the Archery Camp, buried him right next to a wild boar target, and, although I would love to have kept his camera and light, I decided it would work against me if I ever was questioned, so I dumped them in a large garbage can on my way back home.

When I got back to my house I turned on the local news. Then it hit me, hit me hard. They had just announced that there were indications that the serial killer they were after from the Rock-A-Hoola deaths was probably a woman. How they came to that conclusion I don't know, and the news station never explained.

Chapter Twenty-One

Los Angeles the City of Party Crashers

I met a guy named Bob Sabaducci at the Consumer Electronics Show. I was hired to walk a new modern treadmill in the fitness section and Bob came by to chat with me …a dozen times. Bob bragged to me he could get into any party he wanted to in Los Angeles. Oscar parties, Emmy parties, Grammy parties, it didn't matter. If Bob had the motivation and wherewithal to go, he would get in somehow, someway. Sometimes he would get a fake press credential; sometimes he would steal a name off the guest list while the security guard wasn't looking; sometimes he would just tell them he was so and so, a person whose name he was sure was on the guest list. Sometimes he would just walk in with another guest and pretend he was part of their group. And this one I really liked. He would walk in with a full glass of champagne as if he had already been at the party and was just coming back from his car.

Bob promised to take me to a big Hollywood party if I came to town. I told him, I wasn't interested in a party at a hotel or club. I wanted a house party given in an upscale house by an actor, singer, agent or just some rich dude with a big house. He said he could make it happen but it would probably be on a day or two notice.

Bob gave me two days' notice and told me they were going to crash a "Robert Palmer" party in Beverly Hills given by a rich guy named Mick Mickterino who flaunted how great his parties were, and how all his friends loved him, and how they called him the GOAT, Greatest Of All Time.

"I'll bet his friends love him for two reasons, because he throws big parties and because they get invited. The day he stops having parties is the day he's going to lose most of those friends," I said to Bob.

"I think you're right on," he said. "We shouldn't have any problem crashing this party. If you are dressed the right way, no problem getting in."

I drove to LA, checked into a hotel because I didn't want to stay at Bob's house, and met up with Bob the next night, which happened to be a Friday night.

The "right way" meant copying the wardrobe from Robert Palmer's famous song/video Addicted to Love. All the men would be wearing black suits and all the women would be in tight black dresses with their hair pulled back and a lot of red lipstick on their lips.

They didn't even ask for our name. We looked the part and went in. It didn't seem like anybody got turned away, even a guy who wore paisley pants, brought a golf club and told the guy at the door he thought this was an "Arnold Palmer" party.

Mickterino's house was gaudy. A lot of stupid statues, a lot of opulence, including a garage for five cars. Stripper's pole in the basement. But one nice touch was the food. Naked female body covered with sushi. I had seen something similar in at least two TV shows but it was still interesting to see.

I could have dated/killed anybody that night. But I just enjoyed myself and did not accept any of the twelve date offers I received. One thing about LA parties. Most people were single. In Las Vegas, a party was usually coupled off. In LA, a lot of singles looking for that next great guy/girl/husband/wife.

I enjoyed the party. We stayed till 2:00 a.m. and then I asked Bob about the Party Circuit on our drive back to my hotel.

"The Party Circuit is basically a group of acquaintances who communicate among themselves and their sources and usually find parties to crash on Saturday nights. Many years ago you could find parties on both Fridays and Saturdays but these days it's just Saturdays usually. We got lucky tonight because Mictorino usually throws his parties on a Saturday."

"Who are these people?" I asked. "A bunch of insurance salesmen?"

"You are selling them short. A lot of high-end people in this group. Doctors, lawyers, stockbrokers, producers, directors, agents, actors, etc. LA is a big place. You really need this type of network to find the best parties."

"Is I there a leader?" I asked.

"Not really. Some guys have better contacts than others, but nobody is the official leader."

Bob said he had a lead on a party the next night, so he asked me to stay in LA one more night. He picked me up the next night, and fascinated me with information about some people he knew or was familiar with from his life and times on the "Circuit."

"When I say crash a party, some people automatically think this is a rowdy group of people. Not even close. The purpose of getting into a party is to blend in, not stand out," he said.

"The purpose is to become part of the scene, not make a scene," I said.

"You got it," he said.

Bob said there were some good success stories that came from crashing parties.

One guy he knew was a free-lance journalist and became a TV producer. One woman he knew was an executive secretary who was taking acting classes, and she wound up as a lead in a situation comedy.

"Why do you go to these parties?" I asked Bob.

"Two reasons. One, to meet women. Two, to make a business contact. I'm a financial adviser, and I always look for new clients. That's why it's not important I crash the Oscars or Emmys or Grammys. I'm at a party for business purposes."

We stopped at a liquor store and I foot the bill for a bottle of Ketel One Vodka. I was still fascinated by the reasons people crashed parties.

"So are there other reasons people crash parties?" I asked, "Besides women and business contacts."

"Everybody has his or her own criteria," he said. "I know one guy who bases the quality of the party on the amount of food he can scarf down for free. There could be ten Victoria Secret models there and if all they are serving is potato chips and dip, to him it's a lousy party. On the other hand, if they are serving steak, lobster and sushi, but there are no attractive women in attendance, he still thinks it's a great party, and will stay there until they run out of food."

"Who started this Party Circuit?"

"I don't know if history has recorded who started it but there was this one guy who moved out here from New York. He used to befriend people to tell him where the parties were. He would get an address, send out one of his soldiers, and they would report back to him. If the party was good, he would go. If the report was bad, he would keep looking and keep sending soldiers out till he found something decent."

"Now, that guy was smart. He had people do the work for him." I said.

"Well, yes and no. He became so well known, party hosts would give his picture to the security guard with orders not to let him in. Sometimes he would try and fool them by wearing a fake mustache."

"And where is this gentleman today?"

"Oh, he passed away a couple of years ago. I think he was in his seventies. They found him dead lying on his bed nude. He didn't have any friends and he didn't live with anybody, so he was probably dead a good week or two before anybody noticed."

"The guy died in his seventies?" I said. "Was the party circuit his entire life?"

"Pretty much," said Bob. "Ironically, most people are in the Party Circuit to get off it. They want to meet someone and develop a relationship, maybe even marriage. If the relationship goes sour, they get right back on the Circuit."

"And I'm sure some people get so wrapped up in it, they never get off the Party Circuit. They are on it until they die," I said.

"I hope that's not me," Bob replied.

Bob told me we were headed to a party on Mulholland Drive given by a famous rock singer.

In the meantime, he spent much of the drive dissecting parties based on their location within Los Angeles.

"Venice, older smaller houses owned by people who had never got out of the 60s, although it's skewing younger these days. A lot of weed, usually a rock band playing too loud in the living room."

"Beverly Hills, lots of money, more dignified houses, lots of people dressed up. West Hollywood, predominantly gay, of course."

"Westwood, college-age. Downtown, artsy dressed in black. South Bay, money, good jobs, nice compact homes near the water but they never grow up. It's like a return to college fraternity beer keg parties. The Playboy Mansion is probably the ultimate party place."

Bob had it down to a science.

We arrived at a party on Mulholland Drive between Beverly Glen and Benedict Canyon. Nice house tucked back within the trees. We used the name Matt Victor. I didn't know who Matt Victor was but we sailed past security.

Oh my heavens. This was an A-list party. It was given by a famous rock singer who was part of a famous band. A lot of actors, actresses, singers there.

You have to take my word for it. If I start naming names, I think it will come back to haunt me in case I kill someone.

Bob and I went our separate ways at the party. He sensed I wasn't interested in him romantically, so he went out in search of other women.

I was watching these four guys simultaneously covet the current Miss California. I was then approached by a gentleman in his forties, blond hair and goatee. I didn't think he was a lawyer or an actor. I didn't have a guess.

"Are you wishing you were surrounded by four guys, or that you had entered Miss California?"

"I was wondering if she would have won that title without breast implants," I said.

"Maybe her cosmetic surgeon should have shared in her winnings," said Mr. Goatee Man.

"Actually I'm being too catty. I'm not against cosmetic surgery. If it makes a person feel better about their self, it's worth it."

"My name is Matt Victor."

I laughed, "Oh you got in," I said.

"Of course I got in. I was on the list. I'm part of the management company that handles many of these people. Oh wait a minute, you used my name to get in. That's why it was already crossed off."

"No I didn't use your name. But a friend of mine did. I hope you are not offended. He knew you would get in. It was really nothing personal, just random crashing."

"My name is Bri," I said and shook his hand. "Bri Barrington."

"Since you have a knack for sneaking into stranger's homes, I'm going to guess you are a cat burglar, and since you dress well, I'm going to suggest you are a successful one at that."

"Well, I once had a career that took me into peoples' homes but not any longer. I was an interior designer but I couldn't stand the knockdown drag out arguments with prima donna women. So now I'm a promotional model, I set my own hours and I get regular work in Las Vegas."

After spending the next hour talking about the management business and what he does and doesn't do for a client, I accepted his invitation to go back to his house, which was just off Beverly Glen, so only five minutes away. I said my goodbyes to Bob, kissed him on the cheek, and told him we needed to do this again some time.

Matt's house had a hot tub in the backyard. He gave me a red bathing suit to wear. He put on black swim trunks. I went in the bathroom to freshen up as only I know how to and came back out to enjoy the hot bubbly water. We started to kiss. He hugged me. I scratched his back, ever so lightly at first, and then a little harder and deeper. I had put on a special set of fake fingernails to match my own. Beautiful pink color if I do say so myself. Ironically, it was called Poison Pink. Oh, one more thing. These fake nails had a real poison on them, as I guess you could imagine.

Matt passed out with his arms around me. I then put his head underwater for a couple of minutes and he was gone. I got the chills. Another sexual submission for me.

I got out of the hot tub, dried off, went into his bathroom, took off the fake nails and flushed them down the toilet where I knew they would dissolve. I got dressed, wiped off anything I had touched, and I was out the door to meet my Uber driver for my ride back to my hotel.

Chapter Twenty-Two

I Like to Work in Close

Poison is my favorite method of murder. It's easy to obtain, easy to mix in with other ingredients, and allows me to work in close, much like a boxer who knows by instinct when it's time to back off and when it's time to go in for the kill.

I set up my opponent with soft sexual jabs, sweet kisses, massages, maybe even an accidental touch to their groin area. I would sometimes even feign a period of defenselessness and just when they thought I was ready to go down for the count, I would come back with a deadly knockout punch in the form of something poisonous.

Now, here is where I become full of myself. When I have a guy down and out, I just enjoy the moment. It puts a big smile on my face. I feel a sense of benevolence. I am giving my date one last great night to go out on. He is going out as a man with bells ringing, the crowd cheering and his friends in envy. Oh, jeez, what a sicko I am.

My first Vegas kill came when I was still in college. That was the sleazebag priest-in-training who tried to rape me. No remorse. My second Vegas kill—my first as a resident-- came four years later. I had been living here for about a year. It came by accident. And I was remorseful. Now, that's not a word I use often. But it was true.

I met a personal injury attorney, Al Dent. Ambulance Chaser Al I would call him, and we went out a few times until one day he called me to tell me he won $906,000 in the California State Lottery. He asked me out to dinner again. This time we went to Norah's, the best Italian restaurant in Las Vegas, and a good place for locals to go because it wasn't in a hotel.

"I'm going to give up my career as a personal injury attorney," said Al. "The money is good but I certainly don't get any creative satisfaction from it."

"If the money is good, why don't you like it?" I asked.

"Sometimes I feel like I'm cheating people. Not cheating the insurance companies, I really don't care about that. But I felt like I was cheating the guy who hit my client's car. Yeah, he deserved to pay for some damages but sometimes I would ask the insurance company to pay a big price for my clients' pain and suffering, and that would eventually come back to haunt the other guy and probably get his insurance canceled."

"Well, what are you going to do now?"

"I'll sell my practice, then buy a Starbucks franchise or open a Belgian Waffle restaurant called Killer Waffles and enjoy myself."

"Killer Waffles, I like that," I said. "Well, here's to a new life. I think you are going to finally settle down now and maybe even get married."

"Why do you say that?" he asked.

"You can't really make a partner happy until you are happy yourself, and it sounds like you were not happy being a personal injury attorney."

I told Al I had a surprise for him.

"I went berry picking yesterday. You know that new place in Henderson where they sell all kinds of berries, and you can pay a fee to pick some berries."

"Yes, I was going to try that place one of these days." He replied.

"I ended up picking up a bunch. I didn't even know the names of the berries. But there were yellow round ones, red round ones, and dark blue round ones. I went back home, and turned the berries into pies."

"Well, sounds good to me. I can't wait to sample it."

"Well, not sure that can happen," I said. "I'm not the greatest cook, and certainly not a good pastry chef, and I burned the pie crust on all three of them."

He laughed. "Don't worry, I have an idea," he said.

We took off back to my house. I showed Al what remained of my pies. He said no worries, and escorted me to my bed, took off some of my clothes and sarcastically said for me to wait there.

He came back in a minute with a spatula and proceeded to place the berry fillings over my arms, chest and legs. He then took his time, licking and sucking and slurping.

I'd say he was down there a good ten to fifteen minutes.

I guess you could say this was the epitome of working in close.

Finally, he came up for air.

"How was my pie?" I asked him.

"Best dessert I've ever had," he said. "Can't wait to try your home cooking again. Next time, try not to burn it, okay." We talked and kissed for another ten minutes and then all of a sudden Al went into convulsions. His face became distorted. He coughed and gasped for air. Then he just keeled over and died.

I was stunned. I didn't plan this. I added some ingredients to the pies but no poison I promise. Maybe the berries were poisoned at the farm I went to. Or maybe when the berries were heated up, it becomes poisonous. Or maybe he just had a heart attack. I really had no clue.

I started to cry. Just for a minute or so. I was remorseful. I didn't want to call the police. They would still arrest me and claim I was responsible. But once again, when he died, I felt this unexplained surge of power come over me. My self-esteem automatically jumped into high gear. I had an orgasm. Wow, why was this happening?

I put Al in my trunk, drove and drove and drove south on the 15 freeway until I got tired of driving. That's when I saw the signs for now-closed Rock-A-Hoola Water Park.

It would be my first time there. I figured that was as good a place as any to bury poor Al, even if I only had a regular shovel to use and not a motorized one. I started crying again on the ride back home. Just for a few minutes. But I also learned I had a new hobby. A hobby I could get used to. A hobby that made me feel strong, powerful, sexual and put a big smile on my face. Death was looking me in the face, and I was beating it.

Chapter Twenty-Three

Fantasy Kill #1

Do I ever get tired or bored about making the kill? Not really. It's an addiction, I'll admit, so I'm not sure if I can control it to the point of stopping completely. But I do recognize that what starts as a desire turns into a compulsion. I don't feel I have to do the kill. But I want to do it so much that I can almost taste it.

However, I need to take time off once in a while. It's a need to rejuvenate, a need to revitalize myself. A time to shut down and re-boot. I don't want to take a life every week. I take a month or two off sometimes before going back to this kind of pleasure. When I'm not doing a kill, I'm thinking of a person or persons I'd like to kill even if it never happens. I call it my Fantasy Kill.

The thing that pisses me off most, are the killers who randomly kill people in churches, temples, shopping malls, dance clubs, county fairs, schools and one that hit home with me, a music festival in Las Vegas that killed over fifty people, including two girls I had often worked with.

That's one reason I don't believe there is a God because if there is a God, he/she is certainly screwing things up big time.

What pisses me off even more are the empty hypocritical "thoughts and prayers" comments from politicians.

There is only one thing that will get some of these politicians to react. Emotional attachment. In other words, when it hits home, they will feel it. When it becomes personal, they will do more than talk about empty "thoughts and prayers." When there is an emotional attachment to these deaths, that's when we will see some change. For the next two weeks, I vicariously decided that I would try and let these politicians learn about emotional attachment first hand.

I took two weeks off from my modeling gigs and went to Washington DC. I picked out five politicians I would try and set up a meeting with. That proved a waste of time. Not one politician would meet with me. So, I figured I'd try something different.

I went to a gun range for three consecutive days, took six gun classes, then went out and bought myself a Beretta Nano, a silencer, or suppressor as the gun community calls them, and, of course, ammunition. Most of the reliable handguns I researched were in the $400-$500 range. This Beretta only cost me $358. This pistol is small enough for me to carry in a purse, and the guy behind the counter told me it was very reliable and easy to disassemble and reassemble because I'm not the brightest bulb when it comes to taking things apart and putting them back together.

I did my research. So and so, a high-ranking US Senator from the South lived on C Street in the Northeast part of D.C. So and so lived about a block away from him. In all, I found a half dozen gun advocate senators living within a two-mile radius. If I couldn't get a meeting with one of them in their offices, I would see if I could try a more personal touch, their homes. I dressed up as if I was just coming from dinner in a classy Georgetown restaurant. I parked my rental car off C Street and waited for heavy-hitting politician number one to come home. As he rounded his street corner, I held out a pen and notepad and asked for his autograph. Many senators have personal drivers—one of their staff to drive them around during the day. But they are usually on their own at night, going home from the Capitol.

"Please, please, please," I said. "Your wife said you would sign for me. I told her I donated $500 to your last campaign."

"She said it. Then let her sign it," he said sarcastically. He opened up his door and got out of his car, and shook my hand.

"Please," I said. "It would mean a lot to me and my son."

"OK," he said. "How old is your son?"

"Oh he's dead. He was 12. He was shot at Sandy Hook," I said.

Mr. Politician opened his mouth. He was surprised and now a little scared. I pulled out my Beretta and shot the Senator. Once in the stomach and once in the face. He leaned against his car and fell to the ground. I then emptied a third shot into his heart.

I've been told, no one is dead until they hit the ground. I wanted to make sure he hit the ground.

I got into my rental car and drove away. I wonder how this killing will go over the next day.

I then went to the home of Senator #2, also from a southern state, and who just recently organized a "God and Guns" Rally. I drove to his home, and knocked on his door. I changed into a t-shirt that had his name and photo on it.

"Sorry to disturb you sir," I said. "I would just like an autograph. I was at your God and Guns rally and I was so inspired. My son collects autographs of famous people who will go down in history."

"That's very kind," he said. "How old is your son?"

"He would have been fifteen today. He was killed in that Wal-Mart massacre."

"I'm so sorry to hear that. My thoughts and prayers are with you."

After he threw out that meaningless cliché, I drew out my gun and shot him in the stomach, head and one more somewhere as he went down. I then got into my car and drove off.

A mile or so away was a third target. This guy was from Texas. I did the same thing. I pulled my rental car a couple of houses away from his, put on a t-shirt with his photo on it, told him I was a strong supporter, and eventually let it be known that my daughter died at the mass shooting in El Paso. Out came the Beretta, and out came two bullets to the head and one to the gut. Then I drove away.

The next day there was an uproar of course. Three senators dead. Lots of "thoughts and prayers," the flag at half-mast over the Capitol and the White House.

I'm happy to a certain extent when I kill someone in my house but I never use guns. Like I've said, it's a feeling of power, control and to a certain extent sexual satisfaction. It's also the feeling of creatively planning a murder that is different from most others. I'm certainly not mentally ill. I'm totally aware of all my actions. But with these alleged political kills, guns needed to be used. That was the entire point of this, even though it was what I called my Fantasy Kill.

Chapter Twenty-Four

But Wait ...There's More

I'm not a fan of television programming. I love feature films, and sometimes I go to a movie by myself. But television you can have. Except for a few—and I mean only a handful of great shows on HBO and Showtime and some of the streaming services, television is weak. Network sit-coms are just made for dummies. Stupid dialogue, fake laughter, weak plots. Dramas are not much better. I can live through one or two weekly but that's about it. Nothing I'd set my DVR to. No problem, no loss if I miss an episode.

Then you have reality programming. What bullshit. Reality programming is not real. There is a plot attached even though they don't want you to believe it. The producers know that if the reality was real, the audience would get bored. So they put in fake conflict. Really, I can't believe the number of people who watch and believe this crap.

But the worst of television comes either late at night or on weekends. Infomercials. Now, talk about a bunch of crap. Talk about a lack of honesty.

You spend thirty minutes watching these commercials and you feel like you are about to buy the next great product. Only when you get it home, it's not so great after all.

I once bought a non-stick ceramic frying pan that promised the pan would not scratch or peel and that food would absolutely not stick to it. Well, after cooking with it for five weeks, it started to peel. Not just a little. Quite a bit. And of course, food stuck to the pan on almost every occasion.

Then I figured I'd try an ab belt. An ab belt uses Electro Muscle Stimulation and promises to tone your abs into six-pack shape. Not a chance. You may get a little toning from it but you will never—and I mean never—get a six-pack of abs from it without incorporating a diet plan. Even then, don't count on it. The reason this product sells is because people are frickin' lazy. They don't want to go to the gym and exercise, so they figure this gizmo will do the work for them. Dumbshits, and I guess I include myself in this group, because I actually spent over $100 to buy one.

I bring this all up because I went out with an infomercial producer. I met him at an infomercial convention at the Wynn Hotel. I was paid to walk on a treadmill for two days. He was one of the guys that would come around my booth every hour or so to chat with me. His name was Stuart. Older guy, maybe in his fifties. Blondish hair, nice face and about ten pounds overweight. He was staying an extra night in Vegas, and seemed pleasant enough, so I agreed to go out with him.

We had dinner at the Wynn at a seafood restaurant called Lakeside. This restaurant gives you a view of a lake and a wall extending up from the lake and a waterfall extending from the top of the wall down to the water. You could only see the lake and waterfall if you were inside the Wynn property. If you were on the outside looking in, you couldn't see it. Every half hour, a giant frog would appear at the top of the waterfall and sing a song. On this night it was a Garth Brooks song that the frog sang.

I ordered lobster. He ordered filet mignon. And then I brought up infomercials.

"Why do all infomercials lie?"

"I disagree. We have to paint a positive picture of the product or no one will buy it," he said. "There are a lot of good infomercial products out there. I agree, some are not so good, or have faults but most of them are well made."

"The ab belt that will deliver you a six pack? That's bullshit. The non-stick frying pan that won't peel. Bullshit. And that's from personal experience. You guys are just storytellers."

"Oooh, that's too harsh. OK, you have your bad products. I agree. I've done some shows that I can't believe the product works and that people will buy it. But I'm getting paid well to do these and if I don't do it, they'll just give the money to someone else. So I might as well do it."

"Tell me a show you did that you didn't believe in the product," I asked him.

"I did this liquid, a lotion that supposedly grew hair, made from plant extracts. I created a fake story that each of the plant sources came from a different part of the world, and scientists combed the world to find these plants and did years of research before finding the right formula. I figured no one would believe that this stuff would really work. But the show did very well. A lot of people swore by it. A lot of testimonials vouched for it. What can I tell you? I'm just a good producer."

Mr. Producer and I drove back to my house. I threw him on my king size bed. We kissed a little. He fondled my breasts. I touched his crotch. One thing led to another and he ended up pulling out a condom and we had sexual intercourse.

After that I told him he needed to take a bath before I drove him back to the hotel. I told him I had some great bathtub oil he needed to try. I made him go into my bathtub.

Yes, I could have ended it with my "Jaws of Death" Bathtub Dome but that would have been too easy. Fun to watch but I try not to get too repetitive in my kills. I filled up the bathtub with water and I added in my little chemical compound. "Smells nice" he said.

Yes it did. As soon as he got in, the oil kicked in. It soon hit his system, paralyzed his body and he passed out. I lifted his head up, keeping his body still in the water.

I made sure he did not drown. Instead I put an ab belt around his stomach, kissed him on the cheek, and plugged it in. I'm sure he didn't end up with a six-pack but his body was more toned than when our date began.

I waited a half hour, drained the tub, pulled him out and dressed him. It was close to midnight now, very few cars on the road, so I put Mr. Producer in my trunk, wrapped him in a blanket and drove to the archery range. I was running out of these blankets. I use too many of them. I would have to go to Wal Mart and stock up again.

I picked the lock at the archery range once again, drove through the gate, and drove around behind the clubhouse. Found a new wild boar target and buried my friend about twenty feet from it.

I didn't want to bury him right under the target. People who used that target could step on him accidentally and report it to the police.

I drove home, got a good night's sleep, knowing there was now one less infomercial producer around to lie to us, and prepared to take a Southwest Airlines flight to Los Angeles the next morning.

Chapter Twenty-Five

The Opening Act

A friend of mine flew me to Los Angeles to see a reunion of The Buffalo Springfield, whom I was told were popular in the 60s. The group had some big names—Stephen Stills, Neil Young, Richie Furay—even though they were senior citizens by now.

I didn't know much about them but everybody was telling me that their song "For What It's Worth" was a big hit in the 60s and a rallying cry for protestors in those days.

Prior to the Buffalo Springfield coming on there was an opening act called "Who Cares?" Yes, that was really their name. My friend told me that everybody loved this group because they didn't care if anybody loved them. Their one and only hit was a song called "The Opening Act."

"The Arena is Only Half Full

The Fans Are Only Half Aware

The Beer Lines are Long, the Bathroom Lines Longer

They Don't Care

We're an Afterthought.

We're Just the Opening Act."

I loved it. They were playing some good old classic rock and roll and they were making fun of themselves. When they were done, the crowd at the Wiltern Theatre gave them a standing ovation.

After the Buffalo Springfield performed my friend invited me to join him at the after-party in a private room at the concert hall. While everybody else was gravitating toward the headliners, I went over and introduced myself to Skip Skippers, lead singer and founder of "Who Cares?" He looked about fifty-five or sixty, had light brown hair with blond streaks up front, and didn't seem to be damaged by drinks, drugs or the sun.

"I loved your show. You guys got a standing ovation. Well deserved."

"Well, thank you."

"Just another gig for us. But I don't think The Buffalo Springfield will reunite again, so this was special for us as well."

I was curious. "Who else have you opened for?"

"You name it. Rolling Stones, Springsteen, Gaga, Pink, Taylor Swift, a lot of good ones."

"But I bet they all appreciate your music."

"I think they do."

"But somewhere, sometimes you must be the headliner."

"We headline small venues like the House of Blues. But I'm still waiting for the day I can headline a big arena. I guess that's the day I'll feel respected. It's probably not going to happen soon enough, so I'll go into my sixties still being the opening act."

"Like you say in your second verse."

"Exactly," he said. And then he started to sing.

"I'm in the minor leagues,

The sixth round draft choice.

You would rather sit in traffic than see us perform.

We're the Opening Act."

"Do you ever get down on yourself because you are not the headliner?" I asked.

"I have in the past. My psychologist worked me through it. Now I don't care.

"When we named the group "Who Cares?" we meant it. We are getting paid regularly, we are performing nine months every year, and some of my best songwriting has come after I decided life was too short to keep worrying about it."

I probably could have gone back to my hotel with him that night. But I didn't see any need to. It was an enjoyable evening. Why ruin it?

When I returned to Las Vegas I decided to see another shrink. I'm not sure what it would gain me but I thought maybe I'd let someone new take a shot at me. Maybe it would slow down my kill streak.

I set up an appointment under the same rules as all previous psychologists. I'll pay for appointments in cash up front and I'll wear a mask at each session. I tried five male psychologists who turned me down before convincing a female shrink to take me on.

She was good. She brought up questions I had never even thought of. She asked me why I like to be early to every party, every event, every movie, and every date. I told her I didn't really know. I told her I pride myself on being on time.

She told me I have this insecurity that I'll miss something. She said I need to be there early to make sure I can get in ahead of the crowd even if the crowd was not going to show up for another half hour or so.

Why would I care about that? I thought.

She said she thinks I want the crowd to know I'm there; to know I exist. She said maybe the reason I kill so often is that I have to make sure the world knows about me.

"That's not true," I said. "I don't want to get caught."

"Oh one of these days I think you will get caught. It will be your claim to fame. You'll be famous."

"I'm real good at protecting my identity."

"You may slip up one of these days. If you are going to continue to do this, you need to be careful. I mean really careful."

I liked her approach. She didn't tell me I was wrong or that some god would strike me down, or make me feel sorry for what I have done. She just told me to be careful.

On another one of our sessions, she asked me why I chose to be a promotional model instead of a lawyer or an executive. I said I love being in control of my life, my hours, my days of work. I didn't really want to work for someone.

She told me that I felt working for a male boss was humiliating because he had the power, the control.

I agreed. I told her when I first got out of school, I worked for a large corporation, but I was always late, maybe only ten to fifteen minutes late.

"You probably could not distinguish the right your boss had to control your work hours and control you as a person. Again, you felt it was humiliating. Maybe each of your kills is eliminating that humiliation, and showing your boss—whoever that boss may be—that you are the one in control and you are doing just fine, thank you."

I went through the six sessions with her, listened to what she had to say, agreed with her to a certain extent, and decided to let her live.

When I got home after that sixth session, the local news said they couldn't match the DNA they found on the dead bodies with me or any other woman.

I was safe, at least for now. I did not have a prior arrest record, so the Las Vegas police did not have my DNA on file. Or so I thought.

Chapter Twenty-Six

Beauty and the Bear

I was offered $2,500 to do a commercial for an inflatable air bed. The reason I was offered so much—at least that was a lot for me for one day of work--is that I would have to sleep on the bed next to Bam Bam, a 600 pound grizzly bear.

I decided to do it and a few days later I was off to California with a couple of members of the crew ready to sleep with a bear. We drove into Southern California, in a remote area near Palmdale. This was where we ran into a company that trained animals.

A lot of animals. Tigers, lions, bears, horses, dogs, even an elephant. The place, called Animal Plaza, had a half dozen animal trainers on hand, and several more at the ready.

The bear shoot was going to cost the producers about $20,000 because they also needed one shot with Bam Bam and his sister Pebbles on the bed together. This would show how strong the bed was.

We stayed at a local motel a short distance from the location, although no one mentioned that animals known as bed bugs would also be staying there.

The motel reminded me of one of those places you would see on Cops where they surround a room before they catch the bad guys.

The next morning we headed back to Animal Plaza and the head trainer warned us that Bam Bam and Pebbles were not getting along, so he wasn't sure if we would get that shot.

The first set of shots was with Bam Bam. He sat on the bed by himself, he stood on the bed by himself and then I joined him and slept next to him. The head trainer told me that as long as I didn't make any sudden movements I would be all right.

The trainer put a marshmallow in my mouth, and Bam Bam slowly took it out of my mouth and ate it. I petted him, kissed him and got off the bed.

Then it was Pebbles turn. She got on the bed, did some kind of bear exercises on it, and stood on it, making some weird noises. Pebbles weighed about 200 pounds less than Bam Bam but I figured she would still make a formidable opponent for any human that got in her way.

Then came the difficult shot. Both Bam Bam and Pebbles on the bed co-existing.

The bed was strong enough to hold their combined weight. The question was could they co-exist together.

Bam Bam was escorted on the bed first. But as soon as Pebbles got on, she walked right off. She didn't want to share the bed with her big brother. The trainer coaxed Pebbles on the bed again, and sure enough the two started clawing at each other.

The trainer took Pebbles off and decided on a new strategy. He took a feeding tray, poured grape jelly on it, and added a few sugar donuts. These were for Bam Bam to eat and enjoy, and sure enough, Bam Bam slurped them down with no forethought of Emily Post. Once he finished, he settled into the bed sitting up peacefully and calmly.

Now, it was Pebbles turn. But donuts and grape jelly were not going to cut it for this prima donna. Not a chance. The trainer then pulled out all stops and offered Pebbles small bites of cooked rare filet mignon. That did the trick. Pebbles was a diva. She took her time eating the steak and she didn't care what people thought of her. She jumped on the bed, still staying a distance from Bam, and our cameraman got what he needed.

Our day was done. Bam and Pebbles did their shot together. I did my shot with Bam. Time to drive back to Las Vegas.

On our way home we turned on the radio to hear the news. The newscaster reported the FBI had found another dead body at Rock-A-Hoola and was making progress finding the serial killer. The detective said they had some leads and their feeling was still that the killer is a woman.

"I know a guy who works for the FBI," said Steve, our Director of Photography.

"He told me in confidence that they were very close to questioning someone. He said they found some DNA at Rock-A-Hoola that matched a murder that took place in a local hotel about eight years ago."

I didn't say a thing, nor was I even scared they were closing in. Again, why worry twice? I wasn't even living in Las Vegas eight years ago.

*"Oh shit,"*I thought. *"I killed that clergy guy who tried to rape me at Caesar's Palace while I was in college. My first kill. Did they really have my DNA from that night?"*

"But I was still safe." I thought. I had used my given name, my legal last name, Sandstone, in high school and college. I really liked my last name but some ignorant students kept calling me "Sand Stoner" or just "Stoner" and I didn't want to be associated with drugs in any way, so when I got to Las Vegas I legally changed it to something simple, Brianna Barrington.

We got back home, and I needed to think a few things through. I went to the store bought some food, went back home to cook myself some dinner and decided to call Kerrie to ask her if she wanted to meet me for a drink.

We met at The Foundation Room in Mandalay Bay. It would get noisy and loud around midnight but we got there at 10:00 p.m. before the crowd. We found a couch in the corner and I had a Ketel One and Cranberry and she had a Mojito.

"How was your shoot with the bear?" Kerrie asked me.

"Lot of fun. Bear was harmless. He took a marshmallow out of my mouth. I kissed him. Bam Bam was his name."

"When was the last time you kissed someone?" she asked. "You're right. It's been almost a month. I'm due."

"That guy you used to date, do you ever see him?"

"Nope, we've talked a couple of times on the phone. But he has a wife and kid now. I think he still wants to go out with me, even divorce his current wife and marry me, but you know my feeling. When it's over, it's over."

A half hour later, two gentlemen came over, both wearing suits. I guessed they were either lawyers or bank executives. Good guess. One was a lawyer from Delaware; one an executive vice president of a bank in Georgia. Both were in town for a convention and this was the final night.

"So what are you two beautiful ladies celebrating tonight?" asked the bank guy.

"She survived a wrestling match with a grizzly bear," said Kerrie. I then had to explain I was shooting a TV commercial and had to lay on an inflatable air bed with Bam Bam.

I asked the lawyer what kind of law he practiced. He told me—I could have guessed it—personal injury. "Oh so you're an ambulance chaser?" I asked him.

"Used to be," he said. "I guess I've developed enough of a reputation now by referral to make a decent living without having to chase down car crashes at 3:00 a.m."

"Have you started to blast out TV ads?" I asked.

"Not yet. Maybe in the future."

We talked for maybe another hour and I did make a connection with the attorney so I asked him to go back to my home.

I drove us back to my house and we decided to relax on my bed watching a Netflix movie. No sex was planned, although the kissing was pretty decent.

He was in his forties, brown hair, and nice chiseled jawline. Good-looking guy. I went to get some fresh strawberries and canned whipped cream out of the refrigerator. We sat on the bed our backs against the backrest legs straight out. I was barefooted. He kept his socks on. I swirled a couple of strawberries in the whipped cream and placed them ever so slowly in his mouth. I followed each strawberry with a kiss.

About a half hour later, my creative juices were kicking in. I felt I needed to get back into the swing of things. I went to the refrigerator, took a page from the Bam Bam recipe book and brought in some marshmallows. Which I had just purchased that afternoon. Again, I swirled each marshmallow in the whipped cream and put them in his mouth. I teased him a little, twirling the marshmallow on his tongue before letting him digest each one. One. Two. Three. He loved each marshmallow. What I loved was the fact that each had my favorite brand of poison on them.

But this was a slow-acting poison, so I invited him to dance with me. A nice slow romantic dance. I put on a real old oldie, Patti Page singing Tennessee Waltz. Beautiful song with an emotional feel and perfect for a nice slow dance.

As the song was ending, sure enough his breathing became labored and he started choking and vomiting. His eyes grew big, he fell back, passed out on the bed and died.

I kissed him on the cheek, and took a deep breath. It felt good. I needed that.

I then dragged his body into my garage, placed him in the trunk, looked around to see if anyone was watching and began my drive to the archery range. I picked the lock once again at the archery range, drove about a quarter mile up, found a six-foot target of a mountain lion and buried Mr. Delaware nearby. I took another deep breath and let out a "Wow!" The gratification was back, the sexual energy was back. I was back.

✑Chapter Twenty-Seven✑

DEATH FOR DEATH'S SAKE

I'm fascinated by death, not just from personal experience but I'm captivated by graveyards. I remember when I lived in Portland, I took a trip with one of my girlfriends to Seattle and we visited the gravesites of Jimi Hendrix and Bruce Lee. I don't know why but it just captivated me.

That brings me to Randy, a black man about 6-feet-4. I met him while he was attending a trade show at the Las Vegas Convention Center for the funeral industry. He had nothing to do with the business. It was just a subject matter that intrigued him, so he flew over from Denver for a day to attend.

I was hired by a large firm that sold high-end wooden caskets. Some of them had gold around the outside edges of the casket. All of them had a plush interior lining. A soft cotton feel. These caskets were so tempting that if for some reason I was accidentally locked in the convention center for the night, I'd have a good comfortable place to sleep.

Randy walked by my booth, looked at me and took a photo of me seated inside the casket. I had to get permission from the owner to climb inside but he said it was okay.

Any publicity was good publicity. He knew the picture would end up on Facebook or Instagram. I was wearing a black tuxedo and I took my pink heels off so I wouldn't get the casket dirty. Randy said it was his best picture so far.

He then asked someone to take another picture but this one was of me and him. I was in the casket still. He was standing outside it. He asked me to kiss him on the cheek and told the volunteer to take the photo when I kissed him. I surprised him and kissed him on the lips. Click. Click.

"That picture I guess you could say was the kiss of death," he said.

Randy asked me out for a casual dinner and I accepted. We met at Chin Chin at the New York New York Hotel and shared a double order of Chinese Chicken Salad. Chin Chin still calls it Chinese Chicken Salad, not Asian Chicken Salad.

"What's the most fascinating graveyard you've ever visited?" I asked him.

"Pere Lachaise in Paris," he said. "Not even close. Acres and acres of burial sites. Chopin, Moliere, Sarah Bernhardt, Oscar Wilde, Gertrude Stein, and of course, Jim Morrison. The Morrison gravesite is something to see. Here we are in a place full of death and Morrison's burial site is filled with life. People are reading poetry there and guitarists are singing Doors songs. The surrounding gravestones and mausoleums have graffiti written on them.

'You Must Turn When the Music's Over.' 'The End Your Only Friend.' I stayed at his gravesite for over an hour. It was like seeing a part of history come to life."

"Wow, I've never been to Paris yet. But when I go, that's something I will make sure I see," I said.

"How about you?" he asked. "The most interesting cemetery you've ever seen."

"I haven't traveled as much as you, so it would have to be the Hollywood Cemetery. Judy Garland, Rudolph Valentino, Douglas Fairbanks, Tyrone Power, Cecil B. DeMille, Mickey Rooney, George Harrison, Bugsy Siegel and countless others. It fascinated me. I couldn't get enough of it."

"I have an interesting question for you," he said. "How would you like to die? How would you like to be buried?"

"I think I'd like to go out buried in one of my creations. Kind of like the Great Pyramids of Egypt. A lasting monument. Very creative, artistic. After it was built, I would crawl in with my lover and tell the workers to close it up. There would be a plaque on the outside with our names on it, and people would drive from miles around to visit it."

"Oooh, I like that, "he said.

"How about you? How would you like to leave this earth?"

"I'd love to be on the US Olympic Basketball Team. I had just played the game of my life. It's the Gold Medal game. My team, the United States, had come back from a twenty-point deficit, and we are down by one with less than three seconds to play.

The best shooters are covered so the ball comes to me and just as I release it, I am shot by someone in the crowd. I stay conscious long enough to see the ball go through the hoop.

"I hear the crowd cheer, and then I lay down and die."

"Wow," I said. "History in the making."

"Nice stories but I hope neither of these dreams come true," he said.

We then decided to go to a local cemetery on Eastern Avenue. Nothing special, no famous celebrities buried there. We picked a nice grassy area and started to kiss.

"Not the same is it?" said Randy. "It doesn't feel dangerous enough. No celebs. No hiding places. Just a plain old cemetery."

"That's the problem with Las Vegas. For all the famous people who perform here, or who have lived here, you never get the feeling of historical celebrity nostalgia,"I said.

"Nobody goes out of their way to visit a cemetery here. I think the closest you can come is the Neon Boneyard, the resting place of old neon signs."

Just then a security guard comes by, flashes a flashlight on us, and tells us we have to leave.

"Is there somewhere we can go without nighttime security guards?" Randy asks.

"We can go to my place. The only person you have to watch out for there is me."

I drove us back to my house. When we got inside, Randy lifted me up and took me straight to bed. We must have rolled around in bed for an hour or more. Lot of no holds barred kissing and you know the good old fashion sex stuff.

I told him to wait a minute. I had a special after-dinner drink for him. I put on my robe, went to the refrigerator and brought back a decanter filled with Amaretto and two glasses. We toasted each other, but I purposely didn't drink mine. Then I got on top of him, pinned his arms down, and slowly, ever so slowly, released the Amaretto over Randy's lips, in his ear, on his chest and over his groin area.

Randy was turned on to say the least. He put up no resistance. And that was it. The Amaretto was laced with poison, and Randy was gone but certainly not forgotten.

I did cry a little. We had things in common. I didn't have to kill him. But the satisfaction I get emotionally and sexually was too much for me to overcome. My addiction was too much for me to overcome. Death for death's sake.

I remained on top of Randy for a few minutes, still crying a little. I kissed him on the cheek and said softly in his ear even though I knew he couldn't hear me. "This wasn't the Olympics Randy, but the crowd was definitely cheering for you."

Chapter Twenty-Eight

Arguably is a Stupid Word

One of the dumbest words I've ever heard of is arguably. It's usually used by entertainment or sports reporters or commentators. So and so is arguably the best actor on the planet. So and so is arguably the best baseball player of this decade. It's a word that signifies the reporter can't make up his or her mind as to who is the best, and they want to still sound as if they are smart and opinionated and don't want to offend the other players/actors, so they cop out and say that this one person is ARGUABLY the best. Dear stupid reporters, just change the narrative to read, "So and so is ONE OF THE BEST ACTORS/PLAYERS in the business." That's it. No confusion there. You have identified someone as great, one of the best in the world, and that's all you need to do.

Arguably is a word that lets you off the hook and you don't deserve to be left off the hook.

Kerrie and I decided to have lunch at Art's Deli in the Cosmopolitan Hotel and Casino. She ordered a pastrami sandwich on rye with lettuce, tomato and Gulden's spicy brown mustard. I ordered a turkey sandwich on rye with lettuce, tomato and a little mayonnaise.

"This is arguably the biggest deli sandwich in Las Vegas. I know it's the biggest I've ever had. I know I won't be able to finish it," she said.

"You mean Art's makes one of the biggest deli sandwiches they sell in Las Vegas," I said.

"Yes, that's what I said."

"No, you said ARGUABLY it IS the biggest," I said.

"Oh stop it. It's semantics. Yes, Art's sandwiches are among the biggest any restaurant or deli serves in town. Happy?"

"Yes, thank you," I said.

Kerrie wanted to confide something to me, so she turned our conversation into a whisper.

"I had the FBI come visit me yesterday," she said. "You know those dead bodies they found in Rock-A-Hoola Water Park? Well, they seem to think the serial killer was a woman, and somehow my DNA was found on one of the bodies."

"You're kidding me," I said. "What did you tell them?"

"I told them I had never been to Rock-A-Hoola in my entire life and I had never met or gone out with any of the four names they told me."

"What did they say to that?"

"Special Agent Mondale—that was his name, asked me to take a lie detector test, which I did. I was telling the truth, so they thanked me and let me go."

"What happens now?"

"Mondale just told me to stay in town, and they would be back in touch with me if necessary."

"Wow," I said. "You were almost famous. I could have told some of my friends that my best friend was a famous serial killer."

"I don't think I want that accolade," said Kerrie.

"Why did they think it was your DNA?"

"One of the dead bodies had a blanket wrapped around him, and evidently my DNA was on a piece of that blanket."

"Maybe it was one of those blankets you gave away to Goodwill," I said.

"You know what, that's probably right."

We finished our sandwiches, made arrangements to meet later in the week, and said our goodbyes.

"If you are going to kill another one, let me know," I said, "I'd like to watch."

"You are funny."

I had a guess what had happened. Kerrie has slept over at my house a couple of times when she felt too tired or drunk to drive home, so I gave her a blanket and pillow and put her in my spare bedroom. I'm sure I covered one of my victims in one of those blankets. That's why it had her DNA on it.

In the meantime, I felt the FBI was getting a little closer, and that bothered me.

I'm not sure what else I could do. I was careful to wear gloves and not touch the bodies I was burying at the time I was burying them.

But I was worried that my saliva would be on their lips, or face, and I was worried that my first kill at Caesar's Palace back when I was in college would come back to haunt me.

I decided to let off some steam and take my kick boxing class. Only this time I met my match. I was practicing my high kicks and the instructor came over, blocked one of my kicks, swept my other leg, and took me down.

"You may kick high," he said. "But you still need to be careful. You leave yourself open for a block and a counter attack take down."

"You're right." I said. "I need to be more aware."

I decided to do some research as to some self-defense moves and I came upon a hold called The Mandibular Crunch, which was once called The Mandible Claw, which was once called The Mandibular Nerve Pinch. Whoa, this was kinda dangerous. My type of hold.

We can all thank osteopathic physician turned wrestler Sam Sheppard for this hold. Sheppard was convicted of killing his wife in 1954. He spent ten years in prison before a retrial was ordered. He was acquitted in the retrial. He began a professional wrestling career in 1969 under the nickname "Killer" Sam Sheppard at the age of forty-five where he used the Mandibular Nerve Pinch as his finishing hold. He had forty matches before he passed away of natural causes less than a year later in 1970.

The hold stayed dormant until wrestler Mick Foley under the name Mankind brought it out of retirement in 1996.

This hold is applied when I put my middle and ring fingers into my victims' mouths under his tongue, pressing down hard on the soft tissue at the bottom of his mouth. At the same time, I place my thumb or the palm of my hand under his jaw and force his jaw upward.

I asked a friend of mine from class to volunteer his mouth for me. When I applied the hold, he said he felt a painful sensation under his tongue. He had a spasm. My fingers had reached a nerve and it hurt. I told him that if I applied it long enough, he would probably pass out.

"I'd like to see you try this with your bare feet," said my friend. "I'm sure you could get your feet under a guy's tongue."

"Oh, now that would be fun," I said. "But I don't know how long it would take me to work my way into that position. If I needed to use this hold, I'd just as soon get it over with as quickly as possible."

Frankly, I couldn't wait to try this new hold out. And I had a specific person in mind to try it on.

This guy's name was Wayne Talbert, one of those Nazi proponents with a lot of political tattoos on his arms and back who liked to beat up his wives or girlfriends. He killed his first wife and got away with it because she had pulled a knife on him and he claimed it was self-defense. But he had a penchant for using his fists on anybody he dated.

I hung out at the bar I was told he frequented. It took three days before he showed up. I played it coy. I even had a fake tattoo of an American flag glued to my shoulder. I acted very passive. He came over and started to chat. Politics, football, guns, Hispanics, blacks (he used the N word at least twenty times), etc. I agreed with him on everything he said. No arguing. After about an hour, he said he wanted me to take a look at his new truck and then he would drive me back to his house which was only ten minutes away so we could get to know each other better.

We went back to his house, a real dump. I don't think it had been cleaned in months. Beer bottles all over the place.

"What did you do, fire your maid?" I said.

He laughed and then threw a punch that connected with my face.

"Why did you do that? I asked.

"I'm in charge of everything that happens in this house and that means I'm in charge of you," he said. "I want you to take off your clothes now and get into bed. Or I'll beat the shit out of you."

I took off my jeans and heels and was about to walk into his bedroom. I then I did a quick turn around and connected with a spinning back kick to his face. He went down.

I got on top of him and then put my fingers in his mouth under his tongue, and pressed down, and put my thumb under his jaw and pressed up. The Mandibular Crunch was set.

I pressed hard. I didn't want the guy waking up. I kept pressing until he went through three or four spasms, each one more violent than the next. After I was sure he was out, I put his dirty pillow over his mouth and nose and suffocated the bastard. I then raised my arm high and let out a cheer. OK, I'll say it. This was arguably the best kill I had ever made.

ᴄ◞Chapter Twenty-Nine◟ᴐ

Searching for Female Friends

I admit I don't have many female friends. Acquaintances for sure, tons of them. But close gal pals, not really. What makes a true close friend? They will do anything for me and I will do anything for them. Kerrie is my only close female friend. She has my back on anything I do, and I have her back.

There used to be five of us. We would take a trip together every few months. It could be Napa wine country. San Francisco. Los Angeles. San Diego. Even up the road to Mt. Charleston.

After many trips, I got tired of it. Same with Kerrie. It had lost its fun. Same people, same conversations. Whose former boyfriend is screwing whom?; whose husband was trying to close the same business deal month after month after month; No decent guys out there to date; what convention booth you were working at next week. At some point, I kept turning down the trips until they finally got the idea I was tired of it. They stopped asking and I was glad because it was embarrassing to keep turning them down. But I was never ostracized from the group. Some of us would still get together for dinner once in a while, Kerrie and I usually every week or two.

One night it was Janet Dorn's birthday. Janet was a publicist for a local PR firm that was run by an asshole named Mel Kerban, who could always be counted on to tell everybody in the room within the first seven minutes of arriving that he was escorting some celebrity to an event later that week. Kerban was a glad hander. Kissed up to anybody and everybody that could lead him to a potential client. And would always name drop, telling anybody who would listen that he was "real good friends" with a celebrity.

But we all knew that if that celebrity showed up at that very minute, he or she wouldn't recognize Kerban until Kerban went over and re-introduced himself.

Kerban's identity was based not on personal accomplishments but on his association with famous people.

Janet couldn't stand working for him. But he paid on time and it was a good way to get experience so she could one day open her own PR firm.

Janet's birthday dinner was originally scheduled at Blueberry, a trendy restaurant in the Palms that had below average food but was crowded because it attracted celebrities when they were in town. But most of us voted it down because we felt like we wanted quality food over trendy atmosphere. So I suggested another restaurant.

Kerrie and I sat down for dinner with about twelve other people. Aureole at Mandalay Bay was my chosen restaurant.

Aureole had good food and was known for its '*Wine Angels*' who would get into a harness, climb to the top of a large wine rack and pick out the bottle of wine of your choice.

One of the people at my table was a producer for a hidden camera show called Video Avenger. This show was patterned after such TV shows as Candid Camera, Totally Hidden Video and Punked. When Kerrie took off to the rest room, I asked him if there was some way we could play an innocent joke on her. He told me yes, he had something in mind he was shooting the following week. I said count us in. The next day I told Kerrie I had to go to LA for a modeling assignment the following week and I asked her to come with me because all our expenses would be covered.

The practical joke was to take place at a restaurant in Pasadena called Alligator Landing. I had already gone to an "accomplice meeting" at the Video Avenger production offices the day before. Kerrie was considered the "mark." I was the "accomplice." The actors who were participating in the "bit" were called the "plants."

Each segment would be played out if necessary six times. After Kerrie's turn there would be five other women who would go through the same situation. That way when it came time to edit the show for television they could choose the best segment or combine more than one segment into a funny montage.

We arrived at Alligator Landing at our appropriate time, the hostess was also an actress, and she knew exactly where to seat us. The entrance to the restaurant was very clever. You walk over a small bridge and halfway over a mechanical alligator pops up and scares the crap out of anyone who didn't know it was coming.

Rumor has it that when the place first opened, they had a real alligator in the water and it chewed off someone's hand.

After they lost a one million dollar judgment, they built the mechanical alligator. But they figured what they lost in the judgment more than made up for it in the publicity they received. The place has been packed ever since.

Before the server could take our order, I put the joke into play. I pulled out a small vial of perfume, pink in color. This was actually cheap perfume mixed with a little food coloring.

"What's that?" asked Kerrie.

"Perfume. Remember when I went to the Turks and Caicos? Well, I picked up this perfume at a local store, and I never used it. I figured I would bring it out tonight and see if it had any luck for me."

"What do you mean luck?" said Kerrie. "You could get any guy in the world. You don't need luck."

"Yeah but supposedly this is one of those Caribbean love potions. Mixed with the proper body scent it is supposed to make you desirable to any guy around."

"OK, I'll tell you what. Let me be the guinea pig, you are going to get your share of men anyway. Let me test it out," said Kerrie.

Kerrie was actually doing me a favor. I was supposed to accidentally spill a few drops on her. But since she wanted to try it, I didn't need to fake that. "OK, just put a few drops on your wrist, and behind your neck," I said. "Not too much. That little vial cost me $50."

It started to "kick in" immediately. One gentleman walked by our table. He was an actor of course. He did a double take and looked over at Kerrie.

"I'm usually not this forward but I couldn't help but notice you. You are very attractive."

"Well, thank you," said Kerrie. This happened with three more random men in the next ten minutes.

"Maybe that stuff really works," I said.

Our server then came by to take our order. He too was one of the actors. "Have you decided what you want? I do recommend the alligator. It's like a pot roast."

"OK, I'll try the alligator. Don't overcook it, please," said Kerrie.

"What is that perfume you are wearing?" the server asked Kerrie.

"Oh it's something my friend brought back from the Turks and Caicos, and I figured I'd try it out," said Kerrie.

"Well, it smells great," said the waiter. "Are you married?"

"Not anymore since the divorce was finalized," said Kerrie.

After the server left our table, a young attractive gentleman with combed back black hair who was seated at the table next to us kept looking over at Kerrie. After about the fifth time, Kerrie smiled back at him.

"Do you mind if I join you for a minute. My name is Clay."

"You can have a seat until our food gets here," said Kerrie, noticing Clay was almost seated next to her anyway.

"I just couldn't help but notice you. You have a great smile," he said.

"Thank you," said Kerrie. "Are you with anyone?"

"I'm meeting someone. After dinner we are going to go next door and play a friendly game of pool," he said.

"Pool? Kerrie was a college billiards champ" I said.

"Is that right?" asked Clay.

"Three time winner at UNLV," said Kerrie.

"Well, we should definitely play one of these days. I'm not a bad player myself."

Just then our waiter came back. He wasn't too pleased with Clay hitting on Kerrie.

"Weren't you sitting over there a few minutes ago waiting for your girlfriend to show up," said the waiter.

"Aren't you supposed to be handing out menus and cleaning tables?" responded Clay.

Oh this was getting good. The two men were about to square off. The director of the segment then said to me via the bug he had earlier placed in my ear, "Ask Kerrie to step in before they start fighting."

"Kerrie, you need to step in and say something before they get into a brawl," I told her.

"Both of you stop this. There's plenty of me to go around. No need for any arguing or fighting," said Kerrie.

That seemed to do the trick. Clay and our waiter backed off. Then the plot thickened. Clay's girlfriend showed up. "What's going on here? Are you hitting on my boyfriend?" she asked.

"He came over to sit down and talk to us," said Kerrie, now looking somewhat embarrassed.

"I don't like someone trying to horn in on my boyfriend," said the girlfriend, looking for a fight. "Maybe we need to discuss this outside."

"It was all a misunderstanding," said Kerrie. "We just want to have a nice dinner."

"Why do you think this happened?" asked the girlfriend.

"I don't know maybe it's this new perfume I have on. Supposedly it's a love potion," said Kerrie.

"Love potion, I'm sure," said the girlfriend. "No such thing."

"That's what I thought. But this stuff seems to work," said Kerrie.

"Well, I don't care if it works. If you don't stop hitting on my boyfriend, I'm going to settle this with you outside."

Actually, if the two went outside, Kerrie would probably have kicked her ass. She has a brown belt in taekwondo.

"I'm staying right here to eat my dinner. And if your boyfriend or the waiter want to stay here, I'm not going to ask them to leave."

Just then Al Landers, owner of Alligator Landing, came over. "Is there a problem here?" Al was missing a left hand. He had on an artificial hand.

"No problem," said Kerrie. "This gentleman just wanted to talk to me for a minute."

"She's trying to steal my boyfriend," said Clay's girlfriend. "I'm going to rip her eyes out if she doesn't leave him alone." She starts to go after Kerrie.

Al then steps in between the two. "I think I can solve this. That older gentleman at that table in the corner gave me this note to give to you. Please read it out loud."

Kerrie opens the note and reads it out loud. "Congratulations You Are Another Victim of the Video Avenger."

Everybody in the room, all plants, including Clay, his girlfriend and our server, then laughed and applauded.

"You're going to be on TV," said the owner. "There are cameras there, there and there," he pointed out. "You were great."

"Ooh I'm so embarrassed," said Kerrie. "Did you know about this?"

"Of course I did," I said. "Who do you think set it up?"

Kerrie then walked up to one of the cameras that had been secretly hidden behind the waiter's water station. "Hi Mom. I just made a fool of myself. Tell all my relatives I'm really not that stupid." The group then continued to laugh and applaud. And a good time was had by all. I'll do anything for my best friend.

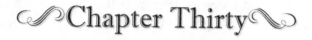

Chapter Thirty

What's a Friend For

I am proud of my sudden death creations. The Barney's Beanery bartender is a work of genius. The lock-down bathtub dome also brilliant. I have studied tortuous creations, works of art I call them. Of course, the rack was a good one. Your subject is tied up at all four corners. Both wrists, both ankles. Stretch him and stretch him some more. He's spread eagle until he's basically castrated.

But there is an ancient torture creation that takes that one better. It's called The Scavenger's Daughter. It's the complete opposite of the rack. My prisoner's body is folded into thirds, so to speak. His shins fold up to his thighs and his thighs fold up against his stomach. My prisoner is then locked inside that machine, forcing his body into a human compression. It's pretty severe, and the prisoner will probably die from the compression on his chest eventually.

I have one person in mind for this kind of torture. Kerrie's former husband. This asshole would hit Kerrie at least once a day. When not hitting her, he would abuse her verbally.

That's the main reason Kerrie took up Taekwondo—to defend herself. But the first time she tried to kick him; he beat the shit out of her, enough to send her to the hospital. She called me and I sat with her, and took her home to my house to sleep.

The next day Kerrie filed for divorce. And filed a restraining order at the same time. They have been officially divorced now for almost a year.

I wanted to end this jerk's life once and for all. I knew he was on Seeking Sugar Daddy.Com. I sent a message I was interested and he responded that he would be interested in getting together. He more or less knew what I looked like, so I had to disguise myself. I put on a red wig and glasses and changed my voice pattern into a sweet Southern Belle.

We met at a Japanese restaurant called Kobayashi Bullet. The restaurant was divided into two sections. The Japanese/American section I'll call it. There were holes in the floor under long ground-level tables, so a person can stick his or her legs under the table and pretend this was actually a Japanese restaurant. The other section was the realistic Japanese section. Individual tables on the ground. Pillows to sit on. I chose the Japanese section, and took my heels off before sitting down.

"So what kind of business are you in?" I asked.

"Import-Export. High end furniture and TVs but once in a while I get a selection of Rolex watches,"he said.

I knew that was bullshit. Kerrie had told me long ago that his watches were all fakes.

"What business are you in? He asked.

149

I didn't want to say I was a promotional model. I didn't want to take the chance he would recognize me.

"I'm an interior designer," I said. "I just finished a high rise condo at Panorama Towers, so now I'm unemployed until somebody comes along to hire me."

"I'm always looking for people who can sell my stuff," he said. "I pay a great commission."

"I'm fine for right now. But thanks for the offer."

I didn't want to be with this guy any longer than I had to, so after dinner I suggested we go back to my house. I told him to take off his clothes down to his underwear and I would give him a real treat. He laid down on the bed, I sat on top of him, rolled my fingers around his lips, and then put my fingers in his mouth under his tongue, The Mandibular Crunch once again. He convulsed and convulsed. I told him, "This was for Kerrie." He passed out.

I tried to figure out how to put his body into the Scavenger's Daughter torture chamber, which I had someone make for me. But it was too hard to move his body into those shapes. So I gave up, and just put a plastic bag over his head. Not the creative finish I wanted but the results were just the same.

After he had passed away, I drove once again to the Las Vegas Archery Range, found another animal target about a half mile up the hill, walked about twenty feet from it, and buried the bastard.

This was for Kerrie, although if she ever found out how her ex had died, I would never tell her it was me. That's what best friends are for.

Chapter Thirty-One

I Nailed the Landing

What separates a gymnastics gold medalist from a silver medalist or even a competitor who finishes in fourth or fifth place is often times the landing. In other words, how you finish your dismount. Did you take a step? Did you move even slightly? Or did you nail the landing and stop your body in its tracks without movement.

I came into a similar situation figuratively speaking. Special Agent Alex Mondale of the FBI knocked at my front door. He was about fifty-five or sixty, balding in front, gray hair along the temples. He introduced himself and asked if we could speak inside my house.

"Sure, Agent Mondale," I said. "And this is about what?"

He went on to explain about the Rock-A-Hoola bodies scattered all over that property.

"Have you ever been there?" he asked me.

I needed to be careful here. I needed to tiptoe around this. I needed to nail the landing, nail the story.

"Yes, about a year ago," I said. "A producer friend of mine was planning on shooting a short film about zombies of course and he asked me to go out with him to see Rock-A-Hoola to scout the location. If I had known it was over two hours away, I would have turned him down."

"Was anybody else out there?"

"This older Hispanic looking guy was out there sitting in his car. He seemed to be minding his own business," I said.

"So what did you do out there?"

"I did nothing. I brought out an old blanket of mine and a beach chair and sat there while my friend fired up his drone to get an idea of the overall landscape of the place."

"What did you do with the blanket and beach chair?"

"I left the blanket there. It was dirty. And I took the beach chair back home. I just gave it to Goodwill a couple of months ago."

"So let me guess," I continued. "My DNA was on the blanket, and the blanket was on top of one of the dead bodies."

"Yes, Ms. Barrington you are correct."

"Wow," I said, "I'm a suspect in a serial murder case. Wait till I tell my friends. Seriously, there must be dozens of fingerprints of people out there. You'll have a lot of people to interview."

"I'm probably going to interview five or six females, including you," he said.

"If there are six different people with six different DNA patterns, how can you narrow it down?" I asked.

"Simple. If the same DNA is on more than one body. Let me ask you another question if you don't mind," he said. "Do you recognize any of these photos? Did you happen to go out on a date or work with any of these people?"

He then showed me photos of four different men. Of course, I recognized all four of them. But I told him otherwise.

"Sorry, Agent Mondale, I don't recognize any of them," I said.

I then asked him a question. "How did my DNA come up? I don't think I've ever been arrested."

"Is your real name Brianna Barrington?" he asked.

"That's my legal name, yes," I said. "But my birth name is Brianna Sandstone. I changed it when I moved here because when I was a kid people made fun of it. They would call me Sandstoner or Stoner."

"About eight years ago, you killed someone in self-defense, somebody who was trying to rape you, is that correct?"

"Yes, sir. I was here as a college cheerleader and this guy—an aspiring priest ironically, attempted to rape me. I got the upper hand and accidentally suffocated him. I wasn't trying to kill him, just put him out temporarily. I immediately reported it to Caesar's hotel security, and they reported it to the local police department. My cheerleading coach vouched for me, the football coach and athletic director vouched for me. And the school this guy represented offered to pay me for my anguish. I turned down the money. I just wanted to forget about the whole thing."

"Well, they had your fingerprints on something and that's how we got your DNA," he said.

"I understand. I forgot all about that."

"I'm going to be interviewing a few other women today," said Mondale. "But please stay in town. I'm going to ask you to take a lie detector later this week or early next week."

"OK, I'll be right here. No conventions or trade shows for me this week."

I opened the front door for him and shook his hand as he walked out.

Actually, this was a little unsettling for me. I was a serial killer candidate, and it made me worried.

A couple of days later FBI Special Agent Mondale came back.

"You still want me to take a lie detector test? How about Friday afternoon at 3:00 p.m.?"

"I think that will be fine. But let me get back to you to confirm."

"How about the other serial killer candidates you have spoken with? Are they also taking lie detector tests?"

"Yes," he said. "As soon as I leave here, I've got three more stops to make to set up appointments."

"I need to let you know I'm bringing an attorney with me."

"You have that right," he said.

"I just want to make sure that there are no trick questions. I have no problem answering straightforward questions. Did I kill this guy, or that guy, or whoever. But I don't want ambiguous questions. Does that make sense?"

"Absolutely," he said. "That's fine. By the way, my throat is a little sore, do you mind if I ask you for a bottle of water."

"Not a problem," I said, as I pulled out a small bottle of Fiji water from the refrigerator for him. "You can keep the bottle in case you need an updated DNA sample."

Agent Mondale noticed the Barney's Beanery bartender art piece I had sculpted for me.

"That is great. How did you think of that?"

I explained about the Kienholz Barney's Beanery exhibition I saw in Los Angeles.

"I had somebody make it for me," I said. "I thought it was the most creative art exhibit I had ever walked through."

"Do you mind if I take a closer look?"

"Not at all. But be careful it's fragile."

Sure enough, he went over to it, touched the clock on the face and a vacuum sealed bag popped out and covered his face tightly. He was in panic mode, pulling at the bag with both hands trying to rip it open. But this was a heavy duty plastic bag and it was wrapped too tight.

"I told you to be careful."

I let him panic and when he went to the ground; I sat on top of his chest and suffocated him with my hands over his nose and mouth. "Yes, Detective Mondale, I'm the Rock-A-Hoola serial killer you are after. Good bye."

I took his body, went out to the garage, looked around to make sure there weren't any other FBI detectives around, and put him in the trunk of my car. I then did something daring even for me. Instead of driving to the archery range, my current home for the deceased, I decided to drive back to Rock-A-Hoola. *What an ironic place to bury Special Agent Mondale I thought. Eventually they'll find him.*

On my way back to Las Vegas, I stopped at The Lottery Store, bought myself a diet Pepsi without aspartame, and one lottery ticket, which garnered me zero dollars.

Two days later, another FBI special agent, Stella Kellogg, showed up at my house asking for agent Mondale.

"He was here two days ago. We set up a tentative appointment for me to come in tomorrow to take a lie detector test at 3:00 p.m. But he said he would need to call me back to confirm, and he hasn't done that yet. He said he had three or four other women to interview and then he left."

"We haven't seen him since, and, of course, we're worried," said agent Kellogg.

"OK, just let me know when he comes back and I'll be more than happy to come in for your lie detector test."

"Why don't you still come in tomorrow afternoon," agent Kellogg said.

"OK, that's fine. I am bringing an attorney. I told agent Mondale, he said that was fine."

Once again I explained, I didn't mind direct questions but I didn't want any trick or ambiguous questions.

The next afternoon an attorney friend of mine joined me at the FBI office. I learned how to beat a lie detector test a few years back, so I was confident I would beat it. I learned you cannot show reaction, hesitation, and doubt on the relative questions, the ones they are trying to nail you on. A polygraph examiner I dated once who is still alive today, explained to me on all the relevant questions I should just feel good about myself, as if I were sitting on the beach in Hawaii, listening to the waves roll in. In other words, nice, calm and relaxed. On the control questions such as what my name is I should think the opposite as if I'm dangling on a bridge about to fall off. I should feel nervous.

The polygraph test took less than a half hour, and my attorney found out I had passed. Even though they asked me questions about meeting or dating the four photos they placed in front of me, I did not admit to anything, said I didn't know each of the four men, and that I certainly didn't kill them. I just started daydreaming about laying down in the warm weather on the beach in Hawaii listening to the waves roll in.

The toughest question was when the polygraph examiner asked me if I had been to Rock-A-Hoola more than once. I was nervous on that one. But I took a deep breath, thought about the ocean waves again, and answered I had only been there once.

I walked out of the FBI office with a smile. I had nailed the landing. I scored a perfect ten. I got the gold medal for lying.

"I still would watch that woman," the polygraph examiner told agent Kellogg.

My ease dropping lawyer overheard this. "She may or may not have been telling the truth. But I believe there was some deception there. I believe she had been trained to beat a lie detector test."

Chapter Thirty-Two

PRETTY POISON

I don't consider myself crazy or mentally unstable or psychotic. I feel I am in control of everything I do and plan to do. But if a newspaper were to pigeonhole me, and give me a label like they do all serial killers. I would be "Pretty Poison." Yes, there was a 1968 movie with the same title starring Anthony Perkins and Tuesday Weld but the plot of that movie is nowhere near my life story. I just like the nickname.

I decided I needed a hobby that didn't involve someone dying. I needed something to take my mind off of finding my next victim. I felt I had a knack for painting and I loved art, so I decided to take a special art class. This art class was given by a former graffiti artist who went by the pseudonym Pendry. He was at one time well known and well respected and even had an article written about him in Gentlemen's Quarterly. But these days he's through avoiding the law; not interested in finding new empty spots on empty walls in empty corners of Las Vegas or Los Angeles. He just has a hunger for teaching young students new ways to create art, and, oh by the way, he takes a five per cent cut on anything one of his students sells while they are in his class.

His students can do anything they like. They can use paint, pencil, pen, crayon, lipstick, nail polish, Sharpie markers of different colors, whatever they want. I wanted to paint but I wanted to create a scene using small letters as my brush stroke, so to speak.

My idea was that if you look at my painting from a distance, you would see the entire scene as I wanted you to see it. But if you got up real close, all you would see would be small letters of the alphabet. This would take time because I had to refine my use of painting small letters. Even smaller than this. My scene was a medicine cabinet with all sorts of stuff in it—aspirin, alcohol, ointments, Cortisone, Vaseline, Band-Aids and, of course, in the corner a bottle labeled LP#8, my love potion concoction that many have come in contact with.

I first drew an outline of the inside of the medicine cabinet and within that outline, individual bottles of the various products I would place in there. Then the lettering begins. Little letters "a" through "z." Very time consuming even just to finish one bottle of aspirin. At first the letters didn't spell out anything. Just random letters as each bottle progresses. Then I got bored, so I changed my mind. As I progressed, I decided to spell out certain words. On the Cortisone bottle, I spelled out "no itch."

On the Vaseline bottle, I spelled out "easy slide." On the bottle of alcohol, I spelled out "no pain." On Love Potion #8 I spelled out "serial killer" and "Rock-A-Hoola." I was taking a gamble that someone wouldn't notice the words.

It took me about four months to complete it, just in time for Pendry's Fabulous Showcase, which is what he annually calls it. This is where his students get to sell their creations, and where Pendry makes a little money himself.

160

The Showcase took place at an airport hangar in Santa Monica and I must say there were a lot of creative art designs.

One woman made a large Monopoly board from Popsicle sticks. One man made a wall mural of Pebble Beach golf course using 38,910 golf tees. One woman used small sections of post cards to make a portrait of Abe Lincoln. And one man did a similar scene of Marilyn Monroe, only he hammered nails into a large board to create her likeness.

And then there was one I thought was brilliant. Two artists, one male, one female, both in their thirties, created 45,000 little plastic figures about the height of your index finger. All the figures held their hands over their heads. Then they placed a see-through acrylic floor on top the plastic figures. What it looked like were thousands of people holding up this floor. But they weren't done. They added a pair of women's high heels and men's leather shoes on top of the acrylic floor with just enough of a women's outfit and a men's pair of jeans to be seen. It ended up looking like 45,000 small pairs of hands were holding up the weight of two people. Everybody was impressed with this art piece and it ended up selling for $55,000. I didn't do anywhere near as well financially. My bathroom cabinet sold for $500. I didn't even know who bought it. But about a week later I could tell I was in trouble. I am usually very good about keeping my body count private. No one needs to know, and I never brag about it, or even let on about my hobby. But I later learned that this had been bought by FBI agent Stella Kellogg. And then she called.

"Hi Brianna, this is Special Agent Stella Kellogg from the FBI. " Remember me?"

"Of course I do," I said. "Did agent Mondale ever turn up?"

"Not yet," said Kellogg. "But we're hoping to have some news on him pretty soon. Do you mind if I come over and talk to you once again?"

"Not at all. How about tomorrow afternoon at 2:00 p.m?" I said.

"That's perfect. I'll see you then."

Stella came over the next afternoon and brought with her my bathroom cabinet art piece.

"Did you buy that?" I asked. "I appreciate it if you did."

"No, actually I didn't. They don't pay us enough at the FBI for me to spend a lot of money on art. One of my friends bought it. And she was telling me about how she could see the words even though they were small. When she told me what words she read, I asked her to tell me who the artist was."

"And you put two and two together and figured out I may be a serial killer," I said.

"Just checking out all leads."

"Well, I got bored writing arbitrary letters at random," I told her. "I wanted to have some fun with it. So I started writing words. Yes, "serial killer" was one phrase I wrote, and another was "Rock–A-Hoola." There was really no significance other than I was reading an old newspaper that morning and those phrases came up again and again."

She admired my art pieces, everything from the Barney's Beanery booby-trap bartender sculpture to another drawing,-this one my bedroom set in which I used small letters again. Some of the letters were random, others spelled out sex parts. I had large art pieces and small art pieces. One of my favorites was the Three Glass Apples. One of them was bright red, one Granny Smith green, and one a lighter greenish- yellow. I had put candy in two of them. Green M&Ms in the green apple and red licorice bites in the red apple. The yellow apple would be a surprise to anyone who had opened it up.

"Can I offer you a soft drink or a bottle of water, Stella?" I asked. "And I've got some candy in a couple of those."

"A bottle of water would be great," she said.

I went to the refrigerator and pulled out a small bottle of Fiji. I offered her the green apple. "Do you like M&M's? Only green ones. But there are plain and peanut, your choice. Or how about red licorice. This is a special red licorice that is softer so it doesn't stick to your teeth.

"No thanks," said agent Kellogg. "What kind of candy in the third apple?"

"A little surprise candy I had made up. Something I had custom made." She opened it. And was greeted by another one of my love potion concoctions. I had booby-trapped the yellow apple into squirting the poison liquid right into her face and mouth.

She gagged on the liquid and went down to the ground. It would be over soon I told her. But I would promise to bury her right next to agent Mondale at Rock-A-Hoola. Then she pulled out her gun but I kicked it out of her hands.

"Nice move agent Kellogg. Sorry your FBI career didn't work out the way you wanted."

She grasped her throat, laid down and died.

I then wrapped her up in another blanket, burned the art piece I had created that her friend had bought, and drove to Rock-A-Hoola once again.

I buried her next to agent Mondale just as I had promised. On the way back, I stopped at The Lottery Store, and once again I bought a diet Pepsi without Aspartame, and two lottery tickets.

I got lucky this time. One of the lottery tickets paid me $500. Not the jackpot. But a win just the same. Let's hear it for Pretty Poison. Still undefeated.

Chapter Thirty-Three

The Mashed Potato Guy is a Star

Well, that makes two FBI agents dead. To the FBI, there were now two agents missing. And both related to the same case. I was nervous. The FBI wasn't going to take this lightly. It was only a matter of time before they would want to interview me again.

But tonight, I was looking forward to my date with Paul "Cup Of Coffee" Kilkenny, the former one shot pro baseball player who I met at San Diego Comic Con.

He was taking me to dinner and a concert. He was in town for an insurance convention and wanted to know if I wanted to go to dinner and a Pink concert. He had dinner reservations at the fancy, swanky Joel Robuchon restaurant in the MGM Grand.

I looked at the prices on the menu. "I apologize for asking but how can you afford Robuchon,"I said.

"Well, I sold a big policy to a hotel in San Diego and this is my way of celebrating. I can't think of a better person to celebrate with."

"Well, thank you," I said. "This is a pleasant surprise. How did you know about this restaurant?"

"I was in Monte Carlo a few years ago with a traveling baseball team made up of major and minor leaguers. We were playing a team handpicked by Prince Albert," he said. "We were staying at the Hotel Metropole and Robuchon had a restaurant there. I thought the food was great, and I swore I'd return to another one of his restaurants."

"I feel special that you chose me as your special date," I said.

"Speaking of something special, I want you to find the restroom and report back."

"Yes, sir." I asked the Maître d' and he pointed me in the direction of the library.

I went to the library but I didn't see a restroom sign. But I did see a woman coming out from behind a stack of books. I pressed a button where she exited and that section of the library opened up revealing a sparkling women's bathroom. I was impressed. Hidden bathroom located behind a library wall of classics.

I told Paul I was impressed with the bathroom and thanked him for making sure I experienced it.

I ordered the milk-fed lamb. He ordered the tournedos of beef filet. Both were under $100 each, barely. We started eating and maybe five minutes had gone by and this young waiter comes along with a big bowl of mashed potatoes. And fills up our plates with mashed potatoes.

"I hope you like mashed potatoes," said Paul. "Because he'll be back in about five minutes." Sure enough, the Mashed Potato Guy was back in about five to ten minutes replenishing our plates.

Next time he came back, I asked him if that's all he does at the restaurant.

"Yes, ma'am, this is my full time job here. And nobody is better at making or serving mashed potatoes than me," he said.

I asked him if this was his ultimate job.

"No, ma'am. I want to be an actor. I'm taking classes in the day and I come here for dinnertime. Eventually I will move to LA and try and jump start my career."

'Well, we wish you good luck. And we will tell the manager here that you were a delightful and conscientious mashed potato server and you deserve a raise."

"Thank you, ma'am. I hope you enjoy the rest of your meal."

I asked Paul about his dating life.

"I was too shy when I was growing up," he said. "I couldn't get up the nerve to ask out the good looking girls in high school. Sometimes they would ask me out but then sure enough they would cancel before the date. I grew a pair of balls when I got to college. But I was still shy. Even though I played on the baseball team, I had this introverted demeanor that prevented me from getting dates with the girls I wanted to date.

"It's still like that for me in some places. I'm no good at a bar. If I meet a girl at a party, I'm better because she's not a cold call. She and I presumably have something in common. We both know the person giving the party or a mutual friend of the party giver. It's easier for me to strike up a conversation."

He then asked me about my dating habits.

"I never had a problem getting a date," I told him. "But I was picky. Most girls went for the good-looking jocks. I wanted a guy who had smarts. He had to be decent looking but he had to have a brain. A cool-looking nerd I guess you could say."

I then went on to tell him about my years as a college cheerleader at University of Oregon and about the priest-in-training who tried to rape me and how I killed him.

"Whoa," he said. He then paused. "I'm going to tell you something now that will surprise you. It even surprises me. When you told me you killed someone, it turned me on. I can't imagine me killing someone, and I could never imagine dating someone who did that."

"It turned you on because you have a little bit of submissiveness in you. You want a girl to dominate you, not dominate you in everything you do and every place you go but to dominate you in the bedroom."

"You know what. You're right. I do feel that way at times. How did you feel after you had killed that guy?"

"When I finished suffocating him, I cried. I guess that was my submissive side coming out. I was emotional. Somebody was dead. I had caused that to happen. But after a few minutes that emotion turned into power. I enjoyed the feeling, and the asshole had it coming to him. I think I became a more dominating person after that."

We then walked over to the Grand Garden Arena and saw the Pink concert. We both enjoyed the concert, not only her music and voice but her aerial flights over the audience. In fact, I would say it was one of the most entertaining shows I had ever seen.

After the concert, we went back to my house. I liked Mr. Cup of Coffee. I liked him a lot. We took off each other's clothes except for our underwear and I went to the bathroom to freshen up. When I got out, Paul had a vacuum bag over his head. He was suffocating. He must have touched the Barney's bartender sculpture, and it trapped him. I immediately got a scissors out of my desk drawer, told him to hold still and I cut the plastic bag in front, so he could breathe. He was crying. He fell on the bed.

"I felt like I was going to die. My eyes were seeing panic. My brain was thinking panic. Thank you for saving me," he said.

"I didn't realize you were going to touch that sculpture. I should have warned you not to."

"Why do you have that booby-trapped?" he asked.

"I just do it out of precaution. In case I get people in here that are too aggressive."

We went to bed, and because he liked to be dominated, I stayed on top. We had great sex and we kissed deeply before he left the next morning for his convention. We made arrangements to go out again.

I could have ended his life the previous night just by letting him flounder around with the vacuum bag suffocating him—but I liked him. I had feelings for him. I don't need to kill every guy I date, or even most of the guys I date. I had an emotional attachment to him. If I make an emotional connection with someone, that will save their life in my eyes. Not everybody needs to die.

Chapter Thirty-Four

Tinder Fight Date

I was browsing through YouTube and I came across a short video film about a young girl and guy going out on their first Tinder date. But this was no dinner or drinks date or even a let's jump right into bed date. This was a fight date. The guy and girl meet for the first time and fight each other. Both know martial arts. The girl wins and says "that was fun" in the end as she walks off. Cute.

I thought *why can't I do that? I'd love to meet a guy for the first time and challenge him to a fight. We'd have to be about the same height and weight. What the heck?* I joined Tinder.

I swiped left, left, left, lots of lefts. These were guys who I didn't like for one reason or another. In this case, I wasn't interested in fighting them. I swiped right a couple of times. Saw a few people who were black belts. That wouldn't work for me.

They were too proficient. I'd probably lose.

Then I found a cute guy, my age who was a green belt in one of the karate disciplines.

I made contact with him and he said he would be up for a fight with the idea that neither of us would go all out to hurt someone seriously. I agreed.

We met at a martial arts studio after hours, no one else was there. This was actually kind of cool. It was 11:00 p.m, the small mini mall we were in totally closed.

"How did you get this place?" I asked.

"I know the owner and gave him $50."

"Nice dojo, clean," I said.

We both took off our shoes and bowed to each other before positioning ourselves on the blue mats.

"I'm George," he said.

George was about 5 foot 9, less than 200 pounds. Average build. Nice face, with a two-day beard growth and a tattoo growing down his right arm. Mustaches and beards are ok in my book, but as you already know, tattoos, especially sleeves, are ugly and nothing close to what people consider art.

"Bri," I said and we shook hands. He kept staring at me.

"Wow, you're damn good looking," he said. "I didn't realize how attractive you were."

"Thank you I appreciate that.'

"I've never done this type of date before," he said.

"Me neither. But I thought it would be fun," I said.

"OK, so let's take this a step further. If I win, you go out on a real date with me and buy dinner," he said.

"OK, and if I win," I said. "You have to paint the bedroom in my house."

He laughed and agreed.

We both squared off. He threw a few punches and kicks. Nothing connected hard. I threw a punch and he avoided it. But then I took my left leg and kicked his right knee. It buckled him. He stepped back. And came at me again. I took my left leg again and connected once again with his right knee. He went down. I got on top of him, took his back and put a choke on him. He tapped out.

"Nice going," said George. "Two out of three falls, right?"

"That's fine with me."

He got up, and we bowed toward each other again. And he started to charge me. He threw a punch to my face first, then a punch to one of my breasts, then a kick to my knee.

He wasn't playing around this fall. The kick to the leg was trying to injure me. He was trying to break my knee.

I stepped back, made sure my knee was not injured and signaled him to come at me, which he did.

I took a step back and let loose with my right foot into his groin. He bent down from the pain. I then followed up with a right foot into his jaw. A perfectly placed heel kick. That did it. Knockout. Bri 1, Tinder Guy 0.

I didn't leave him my phone number. Too bad, I really wanted my bedroom painted. I put my heels back on, bowed out of the dojo and shut the door.

I went home, feeling satisfied. But I knew the FBI would be re-interviewing me any day.

I decided to try another Tinder date but a normal dinner or drinks thing.

I found a guy I thought I might get along with, Ralph, and we set up a dinner date at Buddy V's in The Palazzo. This was an Italian restaurant and I had been there once before. The food was pretty good, and not overly expensive. He ordered the chicken rigatoni a la vodka and I ordered linguine and clams. He asked me to name the most unusual restaurant I had ever enjoyed.

"There's a restaurant outside Tulum, Mexico called Kin Toh. Mexican fusion I would call it. And they have private areas they call The Nest. You climb this tree house until you come to the top and there are various private rooms known as The Nest. Each of them overlooks the Mayan Jungle and you get a great view of the Sunset."

"Sounds great," he said. "But how was the food."

"Pretty good, not the greatest I've eaten. But not bad."

"Are you really climbing a tree house?"

"I'm not sure what else to call it? It's basically steps leading up to the various nests. If you look at it from a distance, it does look like a tree house. And one thing that is impressive is the folklore they give you as you embark on the climb."

"Folklore?"

I pulled out a card I had saved and read it to him.

"We are looking for people who want to dream with us, guided by our playful spirit and demands of the Earth. We walk barefoot to remember while our steps move us toward the future."

"Poetic, isn't it?"

"I loved it," he said.

We paused for a minute to continue eating our food.

"OK, now it's your turn," I said. "You tell me the most interesting restaurant you've ever eaten at."

"About five years ago I played in a soccer tournament in Mombasa, Africa, and a nearby beach town had a restaurant called The Cave. The caves were formed out of coral limestone. You are actually eating in the cave. Food was very good. And the roof area was partially open so you got a nice view of the African sky."

"That sounds cool," I said. "I'd like to find something in the US that is just as cool."

He paid the check and we took off back to my house. I knew I wasn't going to have sex with him but some good kissing was on the table. And, of course, one of my surprise desserts.

We were in bed maybe ten minutes, kissing. He had his shirt off and I told him I had a special massage ready for him as well as dessert. I excused myself, went to the refrigerator, and came back with an ice tray fill of colored ice cubes and a large red Popsicle.

I made him turn over onto his stomach and rubbed his back with a few of the ice cubes, making sure I had gloves on to prevent myself from getting cold and, ok I'll say it, getting poison into my system. The ice cubes would take a little time to do their damage.

That's why I created the poison Popsicle. I kissed him on the lips, and followed that by sensually placing the Popsicle in his mouth and slowing swirling it around his tongue.

The Popsicle was made of Love Potion #8 and within about seven or eight minutes, he started gagging and passed peacefully away.

I felt bad for a second. But I really had no emotional attachment with him other than maybe for about ten minutes. To me it was business as usual.

I gathered him up, put him in my trunk, and took a ride to the Las Vegas Archery Range. Once again, no one was around, so I picked the lock. I drove about a quarter of a mile, found a mountain lion target and buried Ralphie right beside it.

What could I say? Another victory, another victim.

ᴄ⁊Chapter Thirty-Fiveᴄ⁊

Rules by Warren Buffet

I nvestor extraordinaire and billionaire Warren Buffett has a rule he says he lives by for financial decisions. He calls it the 10/10/10 rule. How will he feel about his decision in ten minutes, ten months and ten years? If all answers are positive, he goes ahead with the purchase.

I decided to try that rule myself. Not with financial decisions, but with my hobby. If I kill a certain person, how will I feel about it in ten minutes, ten months, and ten years, it was almost like trying to psychoanalyze myself.

After I kill someone, it takes me about fifteen to twenty minutes to wind down. At Buffet's ten -minute mark, sometimes—not always—I feel a little depressed. I have just taken someone's life for no ostensible reason. There will be wives and kids who will miss him. I have cried on occasion. For just a few seconds. Then it's back to reality. My reality.

The kill was planned and I had accomplished what I set out to do. I felt a power come over me, a victory, and this to me was the greatest feeling I have ever experienced.

I guess you could say it was like a high quality sexual experience. But that's not really giving it its fair due. It's more than sexual. It's better than sexual. That's why I can't stop.

At the ten month period, I'm over it. In fact, I usually have forgotten about it in a week or so. I made my move. I did what I wanted to do. It's done. No need to go back and have second thoughts. Same as my rule with ex-boyfriends. When it's over, it's over. Time to move on.

I don't know about Buffett's ten-year mark. I'm not there yet. My first kill when I was eighteen—a little over eight years ago—was made in self-defense. I'm proud of that kill. I relish that kill. The rest of the kills have only come in the past four and one-half years. Most of the men I don't even think about. One or two come into my mind once in a while. What I think about are the ways I have eliminated them. That's the creativity in what I do. That's what makes me proud at times.

The Barney's Beanery bartender booby trap is a work of genius. The lock-jaw closing of my bathtub is a work of genius. Heck, I even liked the poison popsicles I made.

The next day I received a visit from Special Agents Amanda DiGregorio and Phil Locker, both from the FBI. Locker was in his thirties, kind of handsome, starting to bald in the back. DiGregorio was also in her thirties, average looking with a short blonde haircut. It was apparent she was relatively new on the job. She let Locker take the lead.

"Do you remember FBI agents Alex Mondale and Stella Kellogg?" Asked Locker.

"Of course, I do."

"Both of them are missing and both of them had visits with you before they were discovered missing."

"Agent Mondale was over here twice. He said he had other people to interview and we would eventually set up a polygraph test for me," I said. "Agent Kellogg came over here twice also. Once to inquire about Agent Mondale and once to show me an art piece I had created that either she bought or one of her friends had bought. She asked me if I could make her something similar but using her face as the focal point. I told her yes I could and we would get together in a couple of weeks so I could make a preliminary drawing. She left and I haven't seen her since."

"Agent Kellogg told agent DiGregorio that she believed you may be the Rock-A-Hoola serial killer because of some of the words you had written on that art piece," said Locker. "She showed me the words 'serial killer' and 'Rock-A-Hoola' and you became the primary suspect," said DiGregorio.

"I explained to agent Mondale that I had seen those phrases in the paper that morning and I just felt like putting them on the art piece. I was getting bored just putting random letters on my artwork, so I wanted to do something a little different. I told her I would come in for another polygraph test if she wanted. She left and I haven't heard from her since."

"Did she do anything else while she was here?" asked Locker.

"No, she asked for a bottle of water. I gave her a Fiji, she drank it and left."

The two FBI agents left but not before telling me they would see me again. I could tell they weren't going to arrest me because they didn't bring up DNA. I don't think they had my fingerprints on anybody, including the previous two FBI agents I had disposed of.

DiGregorio came back a week later. I could see her pulling up in her car with two fellow agents riding along with her. My fear was that they were going to take me in for questioning or for another lie detector test. I decided I didn't want to stay around and chitchat or be arrested, so I went to my safe place. Yes, this was something I had constructed within a month of moving in.

Underneath an orange and brown tiger stripe rug in my TV room—some would consider it a den—I had built a trap door. Easy to open from the outside if you knew there was a latch on the bottom of a nearby coffee table, and easy to close from the inside. Eventually I had hoped to dig a tunnel out of it to a neighbor's back yard but I hadn't started that project yet. I got inside the safe room, closed the door and waited. I could hear the knocks on my front door. A lot of knocks. I could hear them talking and walking around to my back door and knocking again. About five or six minutes later, they left. I didn't want to take any chances they were still in my yard, or parked in a car right outside my house, so I stayed in my safe little cubby hole another fifteen minutes before I got out.

The next morning, Agent DiGregorio called me and asked me if I would take a drive out to Rock-A-Hoola with her the next day. I told her I would. She came over around 8:00 a.m. I offered her some coffee, she declined and we took off.

Yes, the coffee would have been the end of her.

On the drive out to Rock-A-Hoola, I played dumb. She asked me questions about the landmarks, and I treated it as if I had only been out there once before. I told her I did remember The Lottery Store because I had won a few dollars with a lottery ticket I had bought from there.

We get out to Rock-A-Hoola and she asked me if I recognized anything. I told her, my producer friend drove out to a certain point further out, so he could fire up his drone and get an overall view of the landscape. I told her that when he did that, I just pulled out a beach chair and a blanket and sat down and worked on my tan.

We drove around and then, thinking I was bored and somewhat tired, she says to me out of nowhere, "Is this where you buried most of them?" Of course, she was trying to catch me off guard.

"Ha, ha, that's funny. Nice try," I said. Then I got serious but not angry. "But that's insulting to me. You really think I had something to do with a bunch of murders out here? You need to get your ducks in a row. I'm not your serial killer. I don't know where you manufacture your evidence, but you need to go back to the drawing board and figure out a different approach. I came out here as a favor. I try and cooperate with law enforcement any time I'm asked. But I'd like to go back home now."

Agent DiGregorio took me home. I said goodbye to her and told her if she wanted me to take another polygraph test on another date, to give me a call.

I walked inside my house and I could tell someone had been there. There was an unusual unfamiliar smell. A couple of things on the kitchen table were out of place and my desk inside the den had been tampered with. My calendar was out of place and my laptop had been moved. It was probably the FBI I figured. But if they did get into my computer, they would find nothing. I do not leave any information on my computer about whom I'm dating, or where I go on my dates. The only thing on my computer was a calendar of trade shows and conventions I was scheduled to work.

I then walked inside my bedroom. Bingo. A dead guy on the floor. I put on some gloves. He was from the FBI; his badge said Agent Mike Hartford. He had touched the Barney's Beanery Bartender, which unleashed a vacuum storage bag over his head. And he suffocated. Served him right. Don't touch things that don't belong to you. Oh shit, now I had to get rid of him. But at least Agent DiGregorio wouldn't suspect me. I was with her the entire day. I put Mr. Hartford in my trunk, drove out to the Las Vegas Archery Range, found a new unblemished target of a deer, and buried the man about twenty feet away from it.

Chapter Thirty-Six

The Upside Down Room

I don't know how everything turned upside down in my life. It certainly wasn't planned that way when I was growing up. I wanted to be famous. Not famous as in so-called influencers, who in my eyes are not really famous. Not famous for being reality TV stars who are famous for being famous. I wanted to be famous because I had accomplished something. I didn't need to save the world by killing a guy robbing a bank, or tracking down the once-notorious D. B. Cooper (talk about a guy with balls and creative ingenuity), or winning a seat in the House of Representatives. But I wanted to make my mark on society. Maybe winning an Academy Award for Best Actress. Or A Grammy. Or better yet. Winning a Nobel Prize.

But here I am, a serial killer by choice, but I don't want to become famous. I have no hidden wish to get caught and get my name plastered over TV and newspapers. The known serial killers—Bundy, Dahmer, Richard Ramirez, other sleazebags, are dead. I remember a line in an old movie called The Cincinnati Kid. "What good is honor if you're dead?" Exactly. So I go on with my life, an attractive woman who gets a bunch of promotional modeling assignments; someone who lives in a decent home due to a winning lottery ticket; and yes, a creative sleazebag serial killer. I'm not sure if anyone would be proud of me, including my mother, if she knew what I had become.

I had been asked to do a modeling assignment at the Upside Down House Museum on Hollywood Boulevard. This was actually the former home of Fredericks of Hollywood, a famous store that sold sexy lingerie but is now long gone.

Down the block from the Museum were a half dozen people dressed up as cartoon characters. Mickey Mouse, Spiderman, Superman, Black Widow, etc. They were there to make some extra money getting tips to have a picture taken with someone. I guess this was one way you could say you were making money in Hollywood.

The Upside Down House was really not that impressive to me. They had seven small rooms, about ten by ten, the size of a small office. There was a kitchen, bedroom, bathroom, a kid's room, a laundry room, a room with a bicycle, and a large walk-in closet. Each of the pieces of furniture was, hung, yes, upside down from the ceiling. They were bolted, nailed or in some cases, glued.

I was hired to model for anybody who wanted to take a photo. Most of the photos involved me doing a handstand on the handlebars of a pinkish-orange bicycle that had been bolted to the ceiling, making me look as if I were more or less riding it. One guy wanted me to sit in the dryer as if I were coming out of it. A couple of people had me sit in the bathtub. And one guy had me take off my shoes and he helped me onto the bed that was attached to the ceiling. These photos were more difficult than I imagined because since the props were attached to the ceiling, I needed a ladder and some help to get on them.

Gravity prevented me from actually laying on the bed, so two of the assistants had to hold me out of view of the camera. But what the hell. The museum was paying me $500.

When the place had emptied out, and the manager had shut off all the video cameras, he came over and asked me to lay on one of the right-side-up cabinets with him.

I said I wasn't comfortable with that and I was kind of tired and ready to take an Uber back to my hotel. He said ok, gave me my check, and told me they would love to hire me again one of these days.

My Uber guy arrived in a white Toyota Prius. I told him we were going to the Standard Hotel downtown and we were off. We did not hit any traffic—that in itself was a victory for Los Angeles—and I thanked him when he dropped me off in the back parking lot of the hotel. He asked for my phone number, and I politely declined.

As I was getting out of the back seat of his car, he got out and pushed me back in. He got on top of me and started to punch, and grind. I was prepared. I had some mace spray with me, and I gave him a nice squirt. He called me a bitch but I could tell he was having a hard time seeing. He started to punch again, and after one shot to my face, I put my fingers in his mouth under his tongue and set The Mandibular Crunch hold I had learned in motion. He was shaking and shaking but I wouldn't release the hold. He passed out, I made sure he was tucked in nice and cozy in the back seat, and left him there. This was one dude I would have loved to have killed. Add him to the list. But too many people around and too many questions to be answered at the hotel, so I left him in the back seat alive but in some pain.

Chapter Thirty-Seven

To Live and Die in LA

Back in the days when Playboy Founder and Editor Hugh Hefner was alive, he would throw some great parties at the Playboy Mansion. For women to get invited, you had to send a professional head shot to his secretary and. if approved, you were put on the list. I managed to get invited a half dozen times.

These days, with Hefner passed away, the only real parties you get at The Mansion are to promote something. A liquor company for example would rent The Mansion and invite a certain number of people. If they wanted more women in attendance they would pay extra to make sure several Playmates were on hand,

The main difference between these promotional parties and Hefner parties was the geographical limitations. The promotional parties were only outside. Hefner's parties allowed you to be in the house. Only certain bedrooms were off limits.

On this day, Jack Daniels was promoting its bourbon and decided to throw a party complete with prime rib, Caesar salad, and all the Jack Daniels you could drink.

I randomly sat down at a table and was joined by Russell, a man in his late forties or early fifties, who was a writer for Los Angeles Magazine.

"My name is Russell. I'm a writer for Los Angeles Magazine."

"I'm Bri, nice to meet you."

"Whatever you want, food, drink, dessert, it's on me," he said, hoping I would laugh at his attempted humor.

I gave out a little laugh, and said, "Well, thank you. I'm glad to know someone is watching out for me."

Russell got around to telling me he was working on an article on where famous people had died in Los Angeles.

"I find that fascinating," I said. "Why did you choose that subject?"

"Same reason," he said. "I find it fascinating. And I thought it would be interesting for the reader."

"Have you done a lot of research?" I asked.

"A little. But I am going out tomorrow to look at a few places and take a few photos."

"Ooooh, Ooooh, Ooooh, Ooooh, can I go with you?" I said, reverting into my sixth grade voice. "I will be your best friend."

He thought it over.

I think he was waiting for me to promise him something more.

"I don't know," he said.

"Oh, please. This would be a date I would always remember even when I grow old. You don't know what this would mean to me."

"OK," he said. "But you can't go running off when we get to a location. If you do I'm just going to drive away. I need to be very careful at some of these places because in effect we are trespassing."

"Yes, sir, I promise." And I kissed him on the lips for a quick second.

We started on the road the next morning. First stop was a Hollywood hotel on Franklin. This was where Janis Joplin overdosed on heroin in 1970 at the age of twenty-seven. When Joplin died it was called the Landmark Motor Hotel. Today it's the Highland Gardens Hotel.

Russell took a few photos, and told me he would come back the following week to interview somebody who had some information on the hotel when Joplin was staying there.

Our next stop was Cielo Drive, off Benedict Canyon. This was where the Manson Family murdered Sharon Tate in 1969. You really couldn't get into the property due to the security gate.

"I'm told that the owners tore down the original house in 1994 and built a 17,000 square foot Mediterranean villa on the property," he said.

I told him I saw a footpath that led up the hills behind the property.

"Should we give it a shot? You could get some good photos," I said.

We climbed up the hill, and sure enough we were behind the house.

"You are right. I can get some good shots from here," he said. "Although I wish I did this back in the 80s. My shots would have been of the original house."

He then took me to a few more places. The Chateau Marmont, Bungalow 2, where John Belushi overdosed on heroin in 1982, at the age of thirty-three; a house on Clarkson Road in West Los Angeles where Playboy Playmate of the Year Dorothy Stratten was murdered by her husband in 1980; a house in Beverly Hills on Elm Drive where Lyle and Erik Menendez murdered their parents in 1989; the OJ Simpson house on Rockingham in Brentwood and the condo on Bundy Drive in Brentwood where Nicole Brown Simpson and Ronald Goldman were murdered; an apartment in Santa Monica where actress Margaux Hemingway overdosed on pills in 1996. This was on the same date, thirty-five years earlier that her grandfather Ernest Hemingway committed suicide; a house on Rising Glen Road in the hills above Sunset Strip where actress Brittany Murphy died of cardiac arrest at age thirty-two.

I had to admit. All these locations and stories were fascinating to me.

Our final stop he said he wanted to surprise me. We drove to Brentwood and down a little side street called Fifth Helena Dr. The gate to the property was open.

"That's surprising," he said. "I've been here two or three other times and the gate was never open. Do you want to take a guess who lived and died here?"

"I wouldn't have the slightest idea," I said. "Some famous politician or athlete."

"Marilyn Monroe," he said.

"I got the chills," I said. "You saved the best for last. Let me just take this in for a few minutes. Would you please take a photo of me with the property and house behind me?"

He did and again I gave him a short kiss on the lips.

The sickest part of me—the serial killer in me—would have loved to have buried some of my conquests on Marilyn's property, OJ's property, even the hills above Cielo Drive. That could never happen. But it was a nice thought.

Russell drove me back to my hotel and I promised next time he came to Las Vegas, I would take him out to dinner. That proved sooner than I thought. He was in my hunting grounds in two weeks. I told him I didn't know where all the cool bodies were buried, so it would just be dinner on me.

I chose Blackout, which is promoted as "dining in the dark." They aren't kidding. He was certainly up for it. I picked him up at The Palms and the restaurant was only a short drive from there. Once you enter the dining room, somebody guides you to your table. Eventually your eyes become accustomed to the darkness and you can see your partner. They take your cell phone not because they think you will be rude and look at emails, or answer a spam call. They take the phone because they don't want any stray light in the dining room.

"Did you finish your article?" I asked. "Were you happy with it?"

"I met a guy who had written a paperback book in the 80s about some of the early places people died such as George Reeves, the guy who played Superman on TV, and he helped me in my search," Russell said. "I finished the article last week, and it's due to be published at the beginning of next month."

"Did you go into detail about the properties we visited?"

"Most of them," he said. "I tried to find unusual things about each person or each property. Some were more interesting than others. But overall I was happy with it."

We finished our seven-course prix-fixe menu. They call it the mystery menu. Some of the dishes were a mystery and are still a mystery. The menu changes daily. Price per person is ninety dollars. A little on the expensive side but to me it was worth it and I did owe Russell a big favor. The food was decent. I didn't like all seven courses but it was a satisfying dinner. Supposedly, when you can't see, you other senses are heightened. They promised our touch, taste and smell would improve. I'm not so sure about that but once again the dinner wasn't bad.

I had no plans to end Russell's journalistic career until he asked me back to his hotel room. I said I would join him for a drink. Once back in the room, he was very cordial and polite at first. After two drinks he turned into a different guy. He pounced on me while I was sitting on the bed and laid on top of me humping. But I still thought I could control his desires, so I wouldn't have to kill him.

"Russell, I know you are in love with me, but I don't feel the same away about you," I said. "Can we just be friends and celebrity death buddies."

He sat up. "OK, I'm sorry. That's not really me. I usually don't date women as beautiful as you. I guess I have this fantasy that because I'm a good writer, I can get any woman I want to make love to me and eventually marry me."

"You are a nice guy, and a good writer. But I'm going to be honest here. You are average looking, which is okay. Many times looks aren't important to women. But to compensate for that average look in the mind of some women, you need to make more money.

Articles here and there for Los Angeles Magazine won't make you a millionaire."

"You need to sell a screenplay, or a book or something. Maybe some TV producer will buy the rights to your "Where Celebrities Die in Los Angeles" article, make a TV series out of it, and you'll be set for life."

"You know what? You are right. You hit the winner's button and get to go to the big board for the bonus round. I once went to see a psychologist and she never told me those things. You accurately told me about me in two minutes. I want to thank you for being so honest and for taking me to dinner tonight."

We made arrangements to have dinner next time I was in LA, and I kissed him on the lips again before going out his hotel room door. I was proud of myself for not eliminating Russell's life. He didn't deserve to die. That honor would belong to someone else ...soon.

Chapter Thirty-Eight

Fantasy Kill #2

I don't know much about the Catholic Church, or any religion for that matter, but it pisses me off to no end that the Catholic Church protected pedophiles and other sexual abusers without prosecution.

A report that the Associated Press uncovered, said that through 2018, 1700 priests and clergy had been accused of sex abuse against underage children. The priests had gone largely "unwatched" by the church as well as civil authorities and were allowed to leave on their own. Some wound up in new positions of trust and authority that still put other children into harm's way.

These clergy members wound up as coaches, teachers, counselors, juvenile detention officers, orphanage workers, and one even landed a new job at Disney World. Mickey Mouse and Donald Duck would be proud.

One Catholic school, Don Bosco, which became Salesian High School, had a cluster of abusers for decades. According to CNN, they were protected from criminal prosecution by the school and transferred to other schools and their young victims were pressured and threatened not to report any incidents. The Salesian leaders didn't even report the abuse to the Catholic Church.

According to CNN, the "Salesians are Silencio." In other words, they police themselves on child abuse matters, which means they do nothing. It is with this in mind, that I heard of a former Salesian priest, now in his forties, from Northern California, who had been accused of sexual abuse on several occasions with children under age twelve and after leaving the church "on his own accord," wound up living in Los Angeles and working at of all places, Universal Studios Amusement Park. He was in charge of lining up the kids on a Harry Potter ride. My fantasy said I needed to meet this man.

I paid my entry fee, went into a bathroom and changed clothes into a Flintstones costume I bought and went to the Harry Potter ride, so I could observe him for a couple of hours on two separate days. He would touch boys' crotches, when putting on their seat belts, and then apologize. He did this several times, probably twenty times per day. Once in while I would see him whisper to a little boy, and give him a Harry Potter lollipop, and then once I saw him take one little boy, maybe about ten years old, to the bathroom. I don't know what happened, but the boy came out of the bathroom crying.

On the second day of my observations, when the man was about to go on his lunch break, I told him I needed to see him. I said to him I was an executive of Universal Studios and I noticed him touching young boys. And if it happened again, we would fire him. We already had one complaint.

"It was all a misunderstanding," he said. "I accidentally touched a few boys. I pretty much have to because I put their seat belts on. But it's not sexual. I'll try and avoid it from now on."

"I don't believe a word you're saying but we'll give you another chance," I said.

I then asked him to go inside the executive bathroom with me, which was only about fifty feet from the Harry Potter ride. I told him he needed to read a list of rules and sign off on them. If he didn't sign, we could fire him that day. None of this was real. I had made everything up, and had written the rules myself. Once inside the bathroom, I locked the door. I said this will only take a few minutes and offered him a large yellow lollipop while he read the list of rules. He thanked me, started reading, kept licking, and within about five minutes he had sunk to the floor. I had placed a pretty good dose of poison on the lollipop. I put my hand over his mouth, and pinched his nostrils until he stopped breathing. I then pulled two pig's balls out of one of the pockets in the Flintstones coat I was wearing and put them in his mouth. Real testicles of slaughtered pigs. I went to a special butcher's shop and paid $200 for the pigs' balls. Well worth the price. I left the bathroom, placed an out of order sign on the door, and walked away. A fantasy for sure, but one that would make me happy if it really happened.

I took an evening flight back to Las Vegas and speaking of big balls, the next day two FBI agents showed up unannounced at my front door. Detective Locker and Detective DiGregorio.

"Hello again," I said.

"Another FBI agent is missing," DiGregorio said. "He was reported missing last Wednesday."

194

"Last Wednesday? I was with you wasting an entire day driving to Rock-A-Hoola and back, so if he went missing, it couldn't have been because of me if that's what you are insinuating."

"Well, while you and I were at Rock-A-Hoola, we had him sneak into your house with a court order of course and do a little research. He never returned."

"I don't know what to tell you. There was no one here when I got back but I could tell somebody had been here. My computer was moved and a couple other things were out of place. I sure hope you find him." Like Hell I do.

Chapter Thirty-Nine

The Mob Museum

I was invited to go on a weekend retreat. I guess you would call this a motivational retreat. Maybe eighty to one hundred people in attendance. Surrounded by redwood trees somewhere in Northern California. We would participate in events such as an Indian Sweat Lodge, and take it from me, you sweat big time. There was also some basic Taekwondo instruction, the culmination of which was breaking a board in half with the palm of your hand or the heel of your bare foot. I chose to break the board with my foot.

Then team training took over. We were all divided into teams of ten to try and get over a twenty-foot wall. No ladder, no rope, just us. Fastest time wins. We finally figured it out. We needed to rely on each other, using a boost from our teammates at the beginning. As team members on the ground dwindled, it took shoulders to climb on from the bottom and arms to hold on from the top. Finally, the last man standing climbed as high as he could on the wall and three of his teammates grabbed his arms from the top and helped boost him up and over. We finished third. But honestly we felt a sense of accomplishment that we conquered this as a team.

Then came the tightrope walk challenge. This was cool. You had ropes close together at the beginning and as you walked further, the ropes spread apart. You had to stay on your rope. Once you touched the ground, you were disqualified.

So what we did was pair off, interlocking each other's hands on each side of the rope. As you got further down the rope, the rest of the group sang, "Lean on Me."

We got the picture. We leaned forward on each other and made it as far down the parallel ropes as possible. My partner and I made it almost to the end because we both had long arms and legs. The winning pair were more flexible than everybody else. But no hard feelings. They deserved the applause they received.

One of the guys on my wall climbing team asked me out, saying he was coming to Las Vegas for a convention within a few weeks. I agreed. I try and find new and somewhat unusual or off beat places to set up my kills—I mean my romantic dates. So I came across the Mob Museum in downtown Las Vegas. I could think of no better place to end someone's life than this place.

A few weeks later Lionel came to town. He was in his 30s, curly hair, about six feet tall. He was a personal injury attorney from Santa Clara, California. *What's with these personal injury lawyers? Why do I meet so many of them?* I thought.

I suggested we have dinner at the El Cortez Hotel and then go to the Mob Museum. The El Cortez is a small, older hotel once partially owned by gangsters Meyer Lansky and Bugsy Siegel.

We went to Siegel's 41 Restaurant at the El Cortez. I was told that the hotel pays a monthly fee to the Siegel Estate to maintain the name and photos at the restaurant. The restaurant is known for its prime rib, so we both ordered that. But as an appetizer I made sure we each had a bowl of matzo ball soup. They don't serve cups. When you order the matzo ball soup, you are automatically given a big bowl. I had done some research and there must have been twenty testimonials that the matzo ball soup was "to die for." Sounded good to me. We both tried it, and agreed it was brilliantly made.

The restaurant had a lot of gangster era photos. One stood out to me. It showed Meyer Lansky walking Bugsy Siegel's daughter down the aisle as she was about to get married. The ironic thing about this photo was the fact that it was Lanksy who ordered the hit on Siegel in a Beverly Hills home because Siegel was spending too much money and possibly skimming funds from the Flamingo Hotel he was remodeling.

Lionel and I made small talk. He asked me about modeling at conventions. I asked him if any of his personal injury cases ever went to trial, or do the insurance companies always settle.

"Ninety-nine per cent of my cases are settled," he said. "Insurance companies are usually too lazy to take it to trial. They figure it will cost them more to go to trial, and the personal injury attorneys use this as leverage."

"My problem is the settlement is usually a gouge," I said. "I accidentally hit this woman once at a stop light. Light dent on the passenger side back seat. Clearly a dent but not big at all. I had a dent also and used my insurance to pay for it. This woman lied, claimed she had some bodily injury, and I know she didn't.

In addition to the damage to her car, which she had every right to have covered, my insurance company gave her $14,000 for personal injury. I would have gone to court to say she had no injury but my insurance company did not even bother to research it. They paid the $14,000. I'm sure the agent got at least a third of that."

"Your insurance company felt it would be much more expensive to go to court. Paying $14,000 was no big deal to them."

"Yeah but it's a big deal to me because my insurance company raised my rates the next year."

He switched subjects to our weekend wilderness motivational retreat. He had told me it was his second time going through it.

"I use it to refresh my body and mind," he said. "Did you enjoy it?"

"I thought it was great, especially the lean on me walk and the wall."

Then he did it. He spoiled the evening.

"You have long legs so the walk was perfect for you. But you don't have any strength in your arms, so you should have been one of the first over the wall, not one of the last doing the heavy lifting. As someone who has gone through it before, that's just my opinion."

I paused. A little taken aback but I wasn't going to get into an argument. "Yeah, I agree. I just did what my captain told me to do."

I then suggested we head over to the Mob Museum. The Mob Museum was only a few blocks away and we walked. I was immediately impressed. I thought it was fascinating.

Any mobster you had ever heard of, and, of course, many you hadn't, was there. You learned when they lived, when they died, how they died, and what crime syndicate they were associated with. There were separate sections for the famous St. Valentine's Day Massacre, including a piece of the actual wall complete with bullet holes; the Estes Kefauver Hearings; the Mob's origins in the United States and in Las Vegas; the disappearance and presumed murder of Jimmy Hoffa; and a section on J. Edgar Hoover's reluctance to even recognize the mob at first and instead focus on notorious criminals but not mobsters John Dillinger, Baby Face Nelson, Pretty Boy Floyd and Ma Barker. The museum also offered you a half hour interactive tutorial on crime lab procedures, which I enjoyed.

But if you wanted to know about Al Capone, Charles "Lucky" Luciano, John Gotti, Meyer Lansky, Benjamin "Bugsy" Siegel, Whitey Bulger, any of them, this was the place to educate yourself.

It was getting late. They would close in about twenty minutes. So I had to act fast. On the third floor was a cage for lineups. The FBI would stick five guys in a lineup and hope the witness would identify the culprit. From the witness point of view, you just saw the five guys standing up against a wall. Their heights were noted on the wall. But from the inside—the side where the bad guys stood—they couldn't see who was watching from outside the cage. All you saw was yourself reflected in a mirror. No one else was on that floor, so I went behind the lineup cage and started kissing Lionel. I then offered him a special lollipop, this one small, similar to one your dentist or doctor would give you. I rubbed it on his lips and on his tongue and within a few minutes he was kneeling on the ground before me coughing.

I then put my fingers in his mouth under his tongue and pressed hard, and put my thumb under his jaw and pressed up. I don't know if he heard me but I said, "How is my strength now?" He quivered, spit out saliva, and then laid down in fetal fashion and passed away. I made sure he was lying on the floor, so nobody could see his body from outside the cage. He wouldn't be noticed until the next morning. Another submission for me.

Chapter Forty

A New Piece of Art

There was an empty space in my den that needed filling. My Samsung TV was the centerpiece with the Barney's Beanery booby-trapped bartender on one side and nothing on the other side.

I decided to purchase a red London Telephone Box. Despite a reduction in number the past few years, the traditional red telephone box--it is not called a booth—is still prominent in London. I was told I could buy one for about $1900 including shipping, and it would cost me another few hundred to customize it to my liking.

The first time I had noticed the red phone boxes was a picture in a music magazine showing each of the five original Rolling Stones standing outside one. When I went to London I had my picture taken with one and swore to myself I would own one someday.

I was working the Magic Show. The Magic Show was men's apparel. It had nothing to do with the art of magic. I was hired by Da Vinci Jeans, a relatively new jeans company appealing to younger, slimmer males.

Naturally, they hired two good-looking thin female models to stand at their booth and entice young men to come in and try on a pair. The jeans were actually made in downtown Los Angeles but the owners knew that an Italian name would have better sex appeal and allow them to brag how the jeans were designed in Italy. Not made in Italy but designed in Italy.

The vice president of marketing, Sidney Carducci, asked me out that night. He had heard so much about the Gondola Getaway, had never been on it before, and didn't want to go by himself. I agreed. Sidney was in his fifties, I guessed, about six foot-one with a mustache and long hair.

We ate at Lavo in the Palazzo Hotel, and then headed to the Grand Canal Shoppes where we were met by our gondolier. The Gondola Getaway took about an hour. Our gondolier gave us a bottle of wine, two glasses, and some cheese and crackers. Then he started singing. A little opera. A little pop music. A little Broadway. He was good, I'll give him that, but it was intrusive. If we wanted to have a conversation, we couldn't hear each other talk.

Sidney tipped the guy twenty-five dollars and told him not to sing. The rest of the hour went by quickly. Sidney had tried to kiss me two or three times, but other than a quick peck on the lips, I wasn't into it.

We got to talking about art, I told him of my preferences such as Kienholz' Barney's Beanery installation. He was a Monet fan as well as Dali and told me that at one time there was a great Dali Museum in Cleveland of all places.

"From the 1940s until 1971 this couple displayed their Dali collection out of their home in Cleveland," said Sid. "In 1971 they moved it to another location in

Cleveland, called it a museum, and the opening was attended by Dali himself. The museum is now in St. Petersburg, Florida, I believe."

I had told him so much about my art pieces—the bartender and now the new London telephone box—he asked to come back and see them. I drove us back to my house, and, wouldn't you know it, he pushed me down on my bed, and started to fondle my breasts and kiss me on the neck.

"Can we slow it down please?" I said. "I invited you back to my house because I knew we could have some serious lovemaking. But first please look at my art pieces. This is ostensibly the reason you came over here."

He first noticed the red phone box, made reference to the Rolling Stones photographs that first turned me on to the idea of owning one of these because I had bought a copy of the photo and had it framed.

"Does it work?" he asked.

"Yes, U.S. calls only," I said. "But if you press zero first, you get a pleasant surprise."

Of course that was tempting to him. He got inside the phone box, pressed zero and a spritz of aromatic liquid came out square into his face.

"Smells nice," he said

"Yeah, I chose that scent myself."

What he would soon find out was it was the last smell he would ever take. This was my new fateful booby trap, and I was dying, so to speak, for someone to try it. Sidney laughed at first, then coughed, then had a tough time breathing, and keeled over.

I waited about two or three minutes, and pulled him out. I took his pulse. It was all over. I notched my personal scoreboard once again, and took Mr. Carducci out to the Las Vegas Archery Range for a proper burial. The next day he did not show up at the convention. The owner asked me about him. I said I was with him for dinner and the Gondola Getaway but never saw him after that.

When I got back home, I started making a note. I would burn it but I was just curious how many ways I have killed someone with my creative ingenuity: Barney's Beanery Bartender. London Telephone Box. Bathtub Dome Trap. Three Glass Apples. Strawberries laced with poison. Lollipops laced with poison. Popsicles laced with poison. Fake Fingernails laced with poison. Suffocation often times preceded by my new favorite self-defense hold, The Mandibular Crunch.

Yeah, I am good.

ᒌ⌁Chapter Forty-One⌁ᒐ

Even Superman Can Make a Mistake

After my dates with Lionel and Sidney, I decided I needed a vacation. It wasn't that killing was taking a toll on me. I just needed a break. I wanted to go someplace I had never been before. I had been to Europe twice and loved every city I had a chance to see, so I figured I'd pick out two cities in Europe that I had never previously been to. I chose Budapest, Hungary and Prague, Czech Republic.

Budapest in a way reminded me of Las Vegas. Not the glitz, glamour and neon. But it was Americanized to a certain extent. I could go in a restaurant and feel like I was ordering in any restaurant in the U.S. Steaks, hamburgers, sushi, whatever. And the men and women? They were wide open and seemingly available to anyone interested.

I stayed at the Inter-Continental, right on the water, and within walking distance of the famous Chain Bridge that goes over the Danube River and separates Buda from Pest. I walked over this bridge twice, sidestepping people selling post cards and souvenirs to tourists.

In front of the Intercontinental, six hookers would walk along the public path, but no lie, five of them were the ugliest women you'd ever laid eyes on, and one of them was as beautiful as a Victoria Secret model.

One of the men who was also staying at the Intercontinental was going to a party in town, and he invited me to come along. It was at a club called Bed, and like the name says, there must have been twenty-five beds laying around the premises that took the place of couches, or tables. Each bed had its own female server, and bar back. We chose a bed just a few feet from the water with a great view of the city in the background. I didn't go for the hard stuff on this night. I did a Bailey's Irish Cream and coffee. I wanted to stay awake. I didn't want any stray hands on me.

My companion for the evening, Glenn or Gary or something else with a G, was a guy in his forties. He was in town for an advertising convention. He said he was American from New Jersey but he looked like he had some Asian in him. He was a Scotch man.

Johnnie Walker Gold by choice. Whatever he was good at, it wasn't liquor. After three drinks, he started putting his hands and lips on me. I pushed him away, and politely told him I wasn't interested in having sex tonight. But he kept putting his hands on me, telling me that he invited me, so I was obligated to return the favor.

I didn't have any Love Potion #8 with me, so I resorted to using my now-favorite self-defense hold, The Mandible Crunch. I put my fingers in his mouth, underneath his tongue, and pressed down. My thumb and forefinger went under his jaw and pressed up.

He was in pain. But I kept pressing. Finally he passed out. Without anyone else looking, I rolled him off the bed and into the water. Goodbye Mr. G.

I took a tour the next day of the House of Terror. It wasn't what I had expected. I was hoping to learn some unique new adventurous ways to kill people. This museum was more of a history of Hungary devoted to politics and terror practices during the war.

I stayed an hour and then just started walking local streets. Eventually I came to a shop that would create "custom perfume." The man behind the counter shows you a list of ingredients and you pick what you want.

"Anything that is poisonous when mixed together?" I asked him.

"There could be," he said. "But I am not allowed to influence your decision."

"OK, I understand. Mix me up your most dangerous stuff I said. But I still want it to smell nice and sexy."

He mixed me two vials, one cost me forty dollars, and the other fifty dollars. I'm not sure what ingredients were in them, or why one was more expensive than the other. One of them had a slight vanilla aroma to it, so I named it Vanilla Pest. The other one was floral, and enhancing but it had a slight beer smell. I named it Midnight in Milwaukee. I had never been to Milwaukee. But I thought the name sounded cool and dangerous.

The man behind the counter put a dab of each perfume on his wrists to show me that they weren't poisonous. I thanked him and walked back to my hotel.

I left the next morning for Prague and spent a couple of days playing tourist. Whereas Budapest was a let-it-all-hang-out city, Prague was more controlled, civilized. I got the feeling you needed to get to know people within the city if you wanted to make friends. If they felt comfortable with you and trusted you, they would invite you into their inner circle of friends. I was sorry I didn't plan on staying longer so I just decided to walk around.

Prague has more statues than any other city I had been to. I know Italy has some cities—Rome, Florence—with lots of statues. But those seem to be either religiously oriented or historically oriented. Prague has statues just for the sake of having statues.

They have a statue of literary hero Franz Kafka, and another statue of Franz Kafka's head that spins reflecting the writer's inner torment. They have a statue of a London bus, only this bus has huge biceps like it's ready to pose in a body building competition.

There is one statue that looks like a guy is committing suicide by jumping off a building. It turns out the statue is Sigmund Freud. But the statue I enjoyed the most sits in Wenceslas Square. It's of Superman. Only this Superman didn't stick the landing. His head is in the ground, the rest of his body, costume and all, sticks straight up. If I were an Olympic judge, I'd still give it a nine. It was very clever, and showed me that I needed to watch my step. I needed to take precautions or I'll end up with my head in the ground.

I flew home, and had a wedding invite in front of me. My best friend Kerrie was getting married and she wanted me to be one of her bridesmaids.

I was really happy for her. She had been married once before but the guy was a loser in my opinion. No real job, a crook who sold fake Rolex watches. And he would constantly hit her. They were married two years.

"What did you see in him?" I once asked her.

"When we first met, he was nice. A real gentleman," she said. "He treated me well. He told me he was in the import-export business. That was a lie. He sold drugs and knock off Rolex watches. I'm just glad I didn't have a kid with him."

Kerrie finally got her divorce over a year ago but only after she had to file a restraining order against him because he came after her eight months earlier when she originally filed for divorce.

And as you all know, I took care of him in my own way fairly recently, although I never told Kerrie what I did.

I was happy for Kerrie. Her fiancé is a photographer specializing in portraits of babies and young children. He makes a good living. He enjoys taking her to Vegas Golden Knights hockey games and seeing Cirque shows. And to top it off, she is about to have a baby.

The FBI called to say they are coming by again tomorrow and wanted to know what time I would be home. I told them all morning. Agent Locker showed up by himself. Agent DiGregrio was not with him. I shook Locker's hand.

"Hello Agent Locker, What can I do for you now? Do you want me to drive to Reno with you this time? Look, if you want to have someone go through my house, just ask me. You don't need to go through these charades of getting me to drive somewhere with you."

"No driving today," he said. "I just need to ask you a couple of questions. Have you ever been to the Las Vegas Archery Range?"

"Yes, twice. Both times I was on a date and my date taught me how to shoot with a bow and arrow. One time we shot at a bunch of targets. The other time, we went up a hill and shot at a mountain lion target. And why may I ask do you want to know?"

"One of the members found a dead body out there," she said.

"And you're thinking, that the same serial killer found a new location to replace Rock-A-Hoola."

"Yes, exactly."

"If I recall, you need a code or a key or something to open the lock. And I don't have either,"

"We found some DNA on the body we recovered and we are checking it out now. We may call you back in for another polygraph test next week."

"Any time, just give me a day's notice."

Kerrie had her baby the next week, a boy she named Leo. Leo showed signs of autism, said Kerrie, but they wouldn't know for sure until several months later. I told Kerrie I would help out and I put $5,000 into a trust fund for Leo in case he needed more medical attention.

Kerrie and her new husband chose Caesar's Palace for their ceremony and reception. Caesar's has a wedding chapel just for these occasions. It was a nice affair, maybe 100 people. I didn't' want to go out on a death date with anyone there, although two of the best men asked me out.

Special Agent Locker called me a few days later, and asked me to come in for another lie detector test. I showed up with my attorney friend, put myself in "lying to the lie detector mode" and easily passed the test. But one of their questions had me worried and led me to believe they may have my DNA. That question wanted to know if I had ever found a body or touched a body on the Archery Range grounds. I had to tell them yes, so I made up a story. I told them my date and I went into the clubhouse after our target session and we sat on a couch that was in the shape of a bow. There was a wrapped up sheet on the couch and I sat down and accidentally touched the contents of the sheet and immediately I let out a scream. There was a male body—more of a skeleton really—under the sheet and after I touched it, I immediately got up and went over to another couch.

"Do you remember the names of the men you went out there with," he asked.

"One man was named Phil or Paul. He was here at an insurance convention from San Diego. The other guy was an attorney but I honestly don't remember his name. Both of them were amateur archers and both knew a member, so they were allowed to use the facilities."

Locker called me the following week, and wanted to come over to ask me a few more questions. I said no problem. I had a feeling they were closing in on arresting me. They had been over to my house too many times.

Locker showed up the next morning. He was by himself. I had put on some of my Vanilla Pest perfume. He noticed it as soon as he came in, and said it had a nice aroma.

But in reality it was my toxic Midnight in Milwaukee perfume. I went to my bathroom, pulled out the bottle, and I spritzed him with it. Game over. I had added one poisonous ingredient to the MIM bottle. He deeply inhaled it and went to sleep. Permanently.

I didn't really want another FBI agent to die in my house. That would make four. But I needed to protect myself. I put his body in a blanket, rolled it up and placed it in my trunk. I drove to Las Vegas Archery Range, picked the lock, and found a new deer target to place Agent Locker next to.

◁Chapter Forty-Two▷

They Were Finally Figuring it Out

With four FBI agents missing, I was the odds-on favorite to be named Serial Killer of the Year. Only DiGregorio was left from the original agents who had interviewed me unless they assigned someone else to the case.

Then they finally figured it out. They called the relatives of six or seven of the dead guys and asked them to send personal calendars or computer contact lists or cell phones if they had them. Anything that had to do with dating. After a week or so, they had received information on three of the deceased. On one of them, my name was listed, along with my phone number.

Another week went by and another body was found at Rock-A-Hoola. It was Special Agent Mondale, the first FBI agent who met his fate at my house. No matching DNA could be traced to me but I had a feeling they were ready to arrest me just on circumstantial evidence so I was considering leaving Las Vegas again.

The FBI would need to get approval from the District Attorney's office to arrest me, and that would take a little time because there was no DNA match. Plus, none of the deaths had the same method of murder. Poison, drowning, suffocation, they couldn't get a good handle on it. They needed to get their ducks in a row before arresting me.

I had a dinner date that night with Kerrie. Taka Sushi in a strip mall on Eastern Avenue was our restaurant of choice. The sushi was excellent, reasonably priced and at 9:00 p.m. every night the sushi chefs would perform. Perform? Yep, perform.

All six sushi chefs would line up side by side and the hostess would turn on the Eagles hit song Hotel California. All of them held a wooden sushi board in each hand.

The song had an instrumental intro of about forty-five seconds. At the end of the forty-five seconds, you heard heavy distinct drum beats on the record. At the exact sound of the drumbeats, all six chefs would clack the sushi boards together in unison. That was it. The crowd would applaud and the chefs would go back to doing what they do best.

Kerrie told me about her new husband and that they were getting along well.

"Just don't make the same mistake as last time," I said.

"I vetted him," she said. "I had a private detective do a little research. I think I made a good decision."

"And how's little Leo?" I asked

"I love him with all my heart," she said.

"Are you planning on having a second child?" I asked her.

"Sooner than you think," said Kerrie. "Probably within a year or so. And I want you to be the godmother."

"I'd love to. It'd be an honor."

Special Agent DiGregorio meanwhile received a letter in the mail. "You Are Cordially Invited to Drop Dead." I know this because I received the same one. DiGregorio I'm sure loved being threatened. I did too. When you are threatened, it doesn't scare you. It means just the opposite. It means you were scaring someone.

It was actually just an invite to a movie called "You Are Cordially Invited to Drop Dead" starring a b-movie actor and actress that I had never heard of. It was playing the next night at the Brenden Theatres inside the Palms but I wasn't interested in going.

Agent DiGregorio received something else on her desk. It was the current copy of Las Vegas Weekly. I also picked up a copy. On the cover was a woman's legs barefooted with a dead body next to her. Lying next to the body was a bottle of perfume, a lipstick case and a bottle of poison. The cover blurb read "Killing Them Softly" and the subhead read "Who is Killing Some of Las Vegas Most Prominent Tourists?" The article started out, "At least seven or eight male tourists spent their last night alive in the arms of a beautiful woman who kissed them, probably had sex with them, and then killed them." I liked the opening.

"Although the FBI has separate reports on all the murders, it was Las Vegas Weekly that first linked the now-closed Rock-A-Hoola Water Park as the burial ground for all of them.

"Seven have been positively identified as tourists who came out here for conventions but we are guessing that the Rock-A-Hoola burial site is only a start. We think our Pretty Poison lady found another burial site but the FBI has been blind to uncover it so far. We are guessing another five or six dead bodies can be found at a new location wherever it may be." They hinted at three or four potential burial sites, including the Las Vegas Archery Range, but no confirmations on any of them.

The article went on to say that the FBI has yet to arrest anyone but it had three or four women in mind, and was close to arresting someone. What was interesting that I didn't expect was that these bodies each went through an autopsy.

The Weekly reported that one body had his stomach full of water and strawberry bubble bath. One man had a chocolate covered strawberry in his stomach with a poison liquid injected into it. And a couple bodies, of course, had plastic bags over their faces. Oh, if they could only see my Barney's Beanery Bartender in action, I'd be arrested in less than thirty seconds.

Agent DiGregorio called to say they wanted to talk with me again, and I said any time, just please give me a day's notice. But sure enough they weren't going to give me any notice. The next day she and another FBI agent showed up, so I hid in my secret hide-away again. My car was parked down the block, not in my driveway. She and the other agent knocked and knocked on the front door and the back door and kept knocking for about ten minutes. I stayed hidden for forty-five minutes. I wanted to make sure they were not waiting outside for me.

I felt it was time for me to leave town, so I packed a get-out-of-here-quick travel bag. I would have left town that day except for one major problem that I never expected.

❧Chapter Forty-Three❧

I'm Not Such a Bad Person After All

I cry at everything ...well, almost everything. If I get emotionally attached to a movie, and it has a sad ending or a happy ending, I'm crying. If I watch the Olympics, and someone wins a gold medal, and they are playing the nation's anthem, I'm crying. In most cases it's the Star Spangled Banner making me cry but on some occasions it could be any anthem from any country. This person just spent his or her life training for a sport and they succeeded. That's worth a couple of tears no matter what sport nor what country. And, of course, if I am at a funeral and I knew the person, I cry a lot.

But when it comes to serial killing, I don't cry. I remember crying after my first kill but that went away quickly since the priest-in-training had it coming to him. Very rarely now will I shed a tear after any of my kills.

But then Kerrie's husband Rick called to tell me Kerrie was in an auto accident. The other car with a drunk guy in his early twenties, blindsided her from the driver's side. She was transported to the hospital and was basically fighting for her life.

She had lost one of her kidneys, was on life support and would need a kidney transplant to survive. I immediately volunteered.

If we were a match, I would give her one of my kidneys. I told him to let me know when I could take the test to see if we were a match.

I then hung up the phone and cried like a baby. I cried off and on for two hours. I can honestly say I haven't felt real love in my life except with Justin, the Duck Mascot whom I later became engaged to. None of the men I have ever dated was I in love with. And until now I didn't know what it was like to feel real loss. Nobody in my immediate family has passed away yet. But Kerrie is my best friend and I would do anything for her, including giving her one of my kidneys.

My kidney was a match, so I signed papers allowing them to take one of my kidneys and give it to her. Two days later we were both on the operating table. I learned later there were some complications with the transplant and we both had been very close to death.

I also learned that Agent DiGregorio had stopped by the hospital to question me but I was under anesthesia and in no position to talk. DiGregorio told Kerrie's husband she would be back to see me IF I SURVIVED.

I awoke the next day and so did Kerrie. She thanked me and thanked me and thanked me. I said don't give it a second thought. She was my best friend and I would do anything for her.

A day later they moved Kerrie and me to Intensive Care. We would both need to spend at least two or three more days in the hospital.

The doctor said we were both not out of the woods yet, and wanted to make sure there were no infections or life-threatening complications. Sure enough when Agent DiGregorio found out I had survived the kidney transplant, she came to the hospital to see me.

"I'm glad you are still with us," said DiGregorio. "And I think it was very honorable of you to donate one of your kidney's to your best friend. I hope if something like that ever happens to me, that I will have a best friend as loyal as you."

"Thank you," I said. "But the doctor said I need a few days to recover. It's still touch and go."

"Yes, I know," she said. "When the doctor gives us permission, we are going to arrest you for murder. We are pretty sure you are the Rock-A-Hoola serial killer. I would suggest you get yourself a lawyer. In the meantime, I'm going to have a man stationed outside your room twenty-four hours a day."

"I'm not your serial killer," I told her. "But you do what you have to do. I'll see you in a couple of days."

I wished I could disappear. Buy some invisible dust and poof I'm gone. Maybe I could convince them I was dead. Not literally of course. But In the eyes of the FBI, I wanted to be considered deceased. That wasn't going to happen though. I would never get any doctor or nurse to sign off on that.

But I did have an idea. Maybe I could disappear. I called my friend Tommy Tedesco. He was a magician who goes by the name The Great Thomasino.

I don't know how great Tommy is—he never had a headlining gig at a showroom in Las Vegas—but he is a pretty good magician and would regularly get gigs at clubs or casinos around the country.

Tommy was respected by other magicians. They would sometimes come to him and ask him to create a "trick" or illusion for their show. He was pretty good at that, and the other magicians paid him well for his creativity and knowledge.

I called Tommy and asked him if he could help me. He said absolutely and he would see me the next morning. I asked him to drop by my house, told him where I had hidden a spare key, and asked him to put together an outfit for me to wear once I got out of the hospital, plus bring the weekend suitcase I had recently filled up.

I didn't even recognize Tommy when he showed up. He was dressed in the hospital's janitorial outfit, including a pretty decent fake mustache, and he wheeled in a janitor's wastebasket filled with brooms. This wastebasket was a little wider than the regular one but close enough that no one would notice.

He gave me a beige top, a pair of Seven jeans and some Nike running shoes. I got dressed, then we filled the bed with pillows and blankets, and closed the curtain all around the bed. If anybody asked, Kerrie would tell them the doctor had given me something to help me sleep.

Tommy helped me into his makeshift janitorial basket. We took out a couple of brooms so I would fit but we wanted to leave in a couple to make it look real. Tommy walked us right by the security guard and down the hall into an elevator. We headed to the basement of the hospital, left the janitorial basket in a corner and drove away in Tommy's car.

I stopped by my bank, withdrew $11,000, gave Tommy $1,000 and we were on our way out of Las Vegas. Tommy had gigs lined up in the Pacific Northwest.

Kerrie called me the next morning, twenty-four hours after my escape, and told me Agent DiGregorio was pissed.

She wondered how I got away, yelled at the security guard and put out an all-points bulletin at the airport, the bus station, the train station and nearby hotels.

But we were long gone. We had already arrived in my old stomping grounds, Eugene, Oregon, and I had the itch to make some more deadly mischief. But I was in no shape to do that. I still needed some more rest. It crossed my mind that I may need to be on the run for a while and I'm sure agent DiGregorio would keep looking for me, no matter what city I was spotted in, but that wouldn't stop me from doing what I do best.

Kerrie called me to tell me that Agent DiGregorio was already headed up to Oregon. She found out that The Great Thomasino was the one who had helped me escape and had booked some gigs in Eugene, Portland, Seattle and Vancouver, Canada. They were probably going to arrest him as an accomplice.

I had another idea. I called my one time fiancé, Justin Prestwich. As I've said, Justin was once the Oregon Duck mascot and there was none finer, funnier and friendlier. There were three Duck mascots in a given year all with their own specialties, but Justin was the best and in demand. He was so good after he graduated he ended up getting a job as a mascot for the San Francisco Giants.

When not in baseball season, Justin would teach mascot workshops all over the country. By coincidence, he was in Eugene now teaching Mascot 101. I joined him at Matt Court to see him in action.

People paid $500 to take his weekend seminar. If you were a student at UO, the school took care of it. The class was limited to twelve aspiring mascots and because this was the University of Oregon, the only mascot uniforms available were for The Duck.

It was funny to see eleven Ducks out on the court dancing, doing pushups, sliding, dribbling a basketball, etc. Justin gave me the twelfth Duck outfit.

On the second day of the workshop Agent DiGregorio showed up with another female FBI agent, who introduced herself to the group as Agent Palmquist. We had been working out for about ninety minutes and we all needed some water and a bathroom break. Especially me. With one kidney gone, I would get thirsty fairly quickly.

Justin noticed this and told us each to get a bottle of water out of the ice chest and to hit the bathrooms if we needed to. All the wanna-be-mascots were men so we all went into the men's bathroom, including yours truly. This was a good move on my part since Agent Palmquist stood outside the women's rest room.

By pre-arrangement, some of the guys helped me out the bathroom window, and another guy climbed in the window to take my place. Justin had loaned me his car. I drove to the Eugene Airport, got on a flight to Seattle and another former Duck Mascot Justin had trained who had moved to Seattle and was working for the Seahawks, drove me across the Canadian border.

Now, I'll just do some traveling, sightseeing
little more creative, imaginative, inspired, ar
ingenious killing. I promise you'll hear from me so
guess I better buy a new scoreboard. This one portable.

and a
istic,
on. I

About the Author

Who ever thought that this cute, cool kid would w up to write a novel about a female serial killer? But netimes life takes a strange unplanned turn.

Benjamin Kalb had a background as a sports journalist before heading to television magazine shows as a producer and then off to the world of TV commercials and infomercials as a producer/director/writer.

One of the infomercials he produced and directed, AbTronic, went on to become the top selling show in the world. *"I Belong On A Warning Label"* is his first novel. He is currently working on a second novel. Benjamin graduated with a degree in journalism from the University of Oregon.